THE LAST WALL

THE BEAST ARISES

Book 1 – I AM SLAUGHTER
Dan Abnett

Book 2 – PREDATOR, PREY
Rob Sanders

Book 3 – THE EMPEROR EXPECTS
Gav Thorpe

Book 4 – THE LAST WALL
David Annandale

Book 5 – THRONEWORLD
Guy Haley

Discover the latest books in this multi-volume series at
blacklibrary.com

THE BEAST ARISES

BOOK FOUR

THE LAST
WALL

DAVID ANNANDALE

BLACK LIBRARY

For Margaux, with love and red paint (for speed!).

A BLACK LIBRARY PUBLICATION

First published in Great Britain in 2016 by
Black Library
Games Workshop Ltd
Willow Road
Nottingham NG7 2WS UK

10 9 8 7 6 5 4 3 2 1

Produced by Games Workshop in Nottingham

UK ISBN 13: 978 1 78496 130 5
US ISBN 13: 978 1 78496 161 9

See Black Library on the internet at
blacklibrary.com

Find out more about Games Workshop
and the world of Warhammer 40,000 at
games-workshop.com

Printed and bound in China

Fire sputters...
The shame of our deaths
and our heresies is done. They are
behind us, like wretched phantoms. This
is a new age, a strong age, an age of Imperium.
Despite our losses, despite the fallen sons, despite the
eternal silence of the Emperor, now watching over us in
spirit instead of in person, we will endure. There will be no
more war on such a perilous scale. There will be an end
to wanton destruction. Yes, foes will come and
enemies will arise. Our security will be
threatened, but we will be ready, our
mighty fists raised. There will be no
great war to challenge us now.
We will not be brought
to the brink like that
again...

ONE

Terra – The Imperial Palace

The screams had merged into a single one. On the Avenue of Martyrs, below the Cathedral of the Saviour Emperor, they surrounded Galatea Haas in an infinite variety. Every pilgrim, man or woman, child or adult, rich or poor, was an individual portrait of panic, a soul giving vent to the most profound terror. The entire rich palette of humanity howled around her; some of the shrieks were of pain, and of these some were caused by Haas as she wielded her shock maul, but in the end, all the fear and death blended together into the single collective scream.

'Get back!' Ottmar Kord was yelling, over and over, his voice hoarse with frustration and desperate hate. 'Get back, get back, get back!' Haas' fellow Arbitrator was a few metres to her left, laying into the crowd with the same violence that she was. They were in the midst of a mob turned into a maelstrom. They brought their shock mauls down with such force that they had already killed more than a few pilgrims.

The electrical discharge incapacitated nervous systems, but the physical blows cracked open skulls.

'Get back, get back, get back!'

Get back to where? Haas leaned in to her shield, pushing back against the crush, but she wasn't herding the crowd. There was no line to hold. The nine Arbitrators were scattered rocks in the foaming rush. Their proctor, in a compounding of bad luck, had been trampled in the first moments of the panic. It should not have happened. Morrow was indestructible. He was a wall. A simple mob could not have overcome him. But the multitude, caught in that scream, had been so strong that it had brought him down. The Arbitrators were not restoring order. They were lashing out at chaos.

'Get back, get back, get back!'

Kord's shout was meaningless. The words were just sounds, the raging punctuation of his blows. They were his scream. Haas was yelling, too. She roared at the pilgrims as she struck them down. She hurled her anger at their fear because, like Kord, if she did not, she would become part of the great scream. She understood the fear. They all did.

The universe had betrayed the people. On Holy Terra, where they believed themselves to be most protected by the Emperor's embrace, they looked up and the sky had become the enemy.

The ork moon seemed to graze the spires of the Imperial Palace. It was a monster of rock and metal. The misshapen sphere was all the forms of threat. It was the eye of alien judgement, it was the visage of impossible yet imminent defeat, and it was the fist coming to smash all hope. It should not be. It could not be. And by existing, it threw everything else into doubt.

It was the end.

The waves of the gravity storm shook Terra. The ground rocked beneath Haas' feet. It heaved. Facades crumbled. A hundred metres away, tenements on both sides of the Avenue pancaked, and they and their inhabitants vanished in a cloud of disintegrating rockcrete. The dust engulfed the street in a limbo, then was blown away by the gale winds that had sprung up in the wake of the moon's arrival.

The people ran blind. They trampled those who fell to the heaving earth. They did not see Haas until she beat them down. Some did not register her presence even then. They were fleeing to nowhere, and the only sight they beheld was the star fortress, whether or not they were gazing at the sky.

Haas felt it too. She felt the weight of its being threatening to crush her spirit. If she faltered in her purpose, she was finished. She understood this at an animal level. There was, deep in the frenzy, little room for the rational. She roared again, rammed forward with the shield, and forced the pilgrims before her to fall back three full steps. A tall, corpulent man in finery, some minor aristocrat on his home world, trampled the man and woman in front of him and crashed against her. She smashed her shock maul against the side of his neck. Electricity coursed through his body. His limbs went rigid, vibrating, and he fell on his back.

Behind him, a tenement wall loomed. It was less than ten metres from her. In the middle of the Avenue the sides of the street had seemed an impossible distance away, but the eddies of the mob had pushed her closer to an anchor point after all. The possibility of directed action gave her some focus.

'Kord!' she called. 'The wall!'

She pushed again, making for the tenement facade. She heard Kord calling out to the next Arbitrator, Baskaline, and so the word spread. Her comrades followed her lead. A line began to form again.

The pilgrims numbered in the hundreds of thousands. They could not be dispersed. But Haas grasped at the nebulous idea of breaking off a sliver of the mob, bringing it to heel, and creating a first island of order.

That was barely a plan. The fact that it existed felt like a victory.

Kord, Baskaline and the others battered their way closer. They locked shields with her. One unforgiving step at a time, they pushed towards the tenement. The scream filled Haas' ears. She roared still. She could barely hear herself. She could feel her rage, though, in the tearing of her throat. Hard smash of the shield, swing of the maul, a step, and then again, and again. The facade drew nearer.

Sudden, overturning movement to her left, seen in the corner of her eye. She turned her head. The crowd had upended a vendor's food wagon. Its cooking stove burst, spraying flaming promethium over the pilgrims.

The great scream took on some new notes of pain. The fire spread quickly.

They couldn't hear the scream in the Great Chamber.

There was an official reason given for why the High Lords were meeting in the Chamber's vastness for the first time in years. The hour was a grave one, and called for a return to the most sacred tradition. That was a simple truth. It also had nothing to do with the decision to hold a session here. Vangorich knew of other reasons, some whispered, some not uttered at all. The Clanium Library was still filled with the trappings of Admiral Lansung's vainglory. The Cerebrium, that favoured nest of power plays, was now terrifying. From the top of the Widdershins Tower, the ork moon loomed closer. Even with the casements closed, the presence in the sky pressed upon the room. The Cerebrium was too exposed.

Terror and politics. The Grand Master of the Officio Assassinorum wondered if there was any real difference between the two. The petty wars of the High Lords and their clawing for pre-eminence were the product of fear of each other at least as much as they were of personal greed. Even today, with terror more acute than any of these worthies had ever known in their lives, calculation and manoeuvring did not stop. The orks were on the doorstep of Terra but until they were in the Imperial Palace itself, and perhaps even then, their threat would remain distant. The other Lords were here now. The threats they presented to each other were clear and urgent. The need to neutralise the fraternal enemy never ceased.

And this is why we're here, Vangorich thought. Its walls reinforced during the reconstruction after the Siege, the Great Chamber was the most secure location in which to hold a session, and the most insulated from the world outside. The terrible moon had come, and the ground had quaked, but these walls stood firm. The scream did not reach through them. The High Lords could concentrate on their agendas. They could reduce the threat of the orks and the collapsing order to abstractions – ones that could be discussed and made into factors in personal narratives, not confronted in all their terrible reality.

The Lords took their seats on the central dais. Around them, the tiers of the Great Chamber rose in echoing emptiness. It had been decades since they had been filled. Vangorich could still remember days when the full Senatorum had sat. Hundreds of thousands of people, debates rippling out from the dais and breaking into multiplicities of contention. The process had been messy, often sluggish and frustrating, and it was astonishing that it had worked at all. But it had worked, and worked well. The memories of that living governance sat in accusing silence on the benches, hovered beneath the distant ceiling and its fresco of the Great Crusade, and gathered in the stern eyes of the massive statue of Rogal Dorn.

'You are setting a precedent, Lord Commander,' Vangorich said to Udin Macht Udo after Tobris Ekharth, the Master of the Administratum, had called the session to order. 'Notice will be taken that we are meeting here. Other voices will demand to be heard.' He took some pleasure in reminding the High Lords that the scream would find them here in the end. They could not hide from events. If the Great Chamber was used, it would fill.

Udo wasn't thrown. 'Quite so, Grand Master. That is as it should be, in this time of crisis. They will be heard, in due course.'

Vangorich nodded, expression neutral. Udo couldn't be

thinking of spreading blame for failure, could he? The Lord Commander did understand that failure meant destruction for everyone, didn't he? Vangorich's fear of what was about to befall Terra, already acute, grew worse at the thought that the High Lords were not as afraid as they should be.

'Admiral,' Udo said to Lansung, 'what are your recommendations?'

The question was respectful in its phrasing and its tone. It did not have to sound like an attack in order to be one. The session was being held far from Lansung's trappings of authority in the Clanium Library. Udo wasn't soliciting his advice. He was exposing the Lord High Admiral's weakness, distancing himself from a former ally before he could be damaged by the other man's fall.

'Our options are limited,' Lansung answered. His normally florid face was grey. His generous flesh hung on his frame as if it were pulling him to the ground. He had been brought low at the moment of his triumph. The bluster and calculation had drained from him. Whatever Vangorich thought of him as a politician, he knew Lansung was a brilliant military tactician. Alone among the High Lords, he had fought the orks. He had a true understanding of what had come upon them, and he spoke with a despair born of realism. 'I've ordered the immediate return to Terra of the coreward fleet. But the orks are here now. We have the *Autocephalax Eternal* and its escort, along with those ships that had remained on local patrol and were not destroyed by the gravity storm. A squadron's worth. Not much more.'

'You destroyed one ork moon,' Juskina Tull said. The Speaker for the Chartist Captains had preserved all the glamour of her raiment in the flight from the Praetorian Way. When she had stood with the others to welcome Lansung as a triumphant hero, the beauty of her dress seemed an acknowledgement of the importance of the occasion. Now it gave her an air of command. 'You know how to do it now, don't you?' Her tone was sharp. Vangorich heard in her question the expectation, perhaps even the hope, that Lansung would respond in the negative.

He did not disappoint her. 'The fortress we fought was a fraction of the size,' he said. 'If this one's orbit were as close to Terra as that of the one over Ardamantua, the tectonic upheavals would have been devastating. Meanwhile, our resources are nothing compared to what we had at Port Sanctus. If we launch an attack, the orks will swat us from the void. The least bad choice is a defensive posture. We can hope to hold the orks at bay until our main force arrives.'

We can hope. Vangorich noted the phrasing. An invitation to engage in wishful thinking, and nothing more.

'But the orks could be here within hours,' Mesring said. The Ecclesiarch of the Adeptus Ministorum, Lansung's other ally, now deserted him. 'How long do you expect us to hold?'

'If you know of a way to accelerate warp travel, I'm eager to hear it,' Lansung shot back.

'If the orks have the temerity to land, they will be repulsed,' Abel Verreault said. The Lord Commander Militant of the Astra Militarum was the junior member of the High Lords. Since succeeding Lord Heth, he had been sidelined, his forces given no role to play in the campaign run by Lansung. His pronouncement was met by a few seconds of uncomfortable silence. Everyone on the dais wanted him to be correct. But the orks had destroyed the Imperial Fists in ground combat.

'There is little that can be done while anarchy reigns beyond these walls,' Udo declared. He looked at Vernor Zeck, Grand Provost Marshal of the Adeptus Arbites. They all did. Vangorich sensed an unspoken, barely conscious consensus to shift the spotlight onto Zeck. It was plausible to view the panic as the first urgency. If it was not already worldwide, it would be within twenty-four hours. There was a real risk of a total collapse of order doing the work of the orks for them.

Even so, Vangorich seethed at the naked abdication of responsibility he was witnessing. If action depended on Zeck restoring order, then the other High Lords were absolved of the need to make any critical decisions of their own until the forces of the Adeptus Arbites had quelled the panic.

'No other action is proposed?' he asked.

'There is none to take, beyond the preparation of orbital defences,' Udo said, giving Lansung a significant glance. No one contradicted him.

Zeck did not respond. He hadn't moved since taking his seat. His augmetics were so extensive that he was barely more human than Fabricator General Kubik. Neither had reacted to anything the others had said, remaining statues throughout the session. The Lord of the Mechanicus was an insect-like collection of metallic angles, sensors and tubes. The Provost Marshal was a squat hulk, a machinic and organic embodiment of the necessary violence of the law. He turned his attention from the stream of reports fed to his bionic ear with visible reluctance.

'The situation is fluid,' he said.

'It can't remain so,' said Mesring. 'Disorder is heresy.'

Zeck turned his head to stare at the Ecclesiarch.

'Perhaps you'd like to address the crowds outside?' When Mesring didn't answer, Zeck rose. His awareness had been beyond the Great Chamber, calculating the vectors of perhaps the greatest exercise in crowd control in human history. Now he was realising that the situation had given him the whip hand. The other High Lords had, for the moment, surrendered their agency.

Opportunity, Vangorich thought. You can't resist its scent, can you?

Verreault began, 'The Astra Militarum–'

'Is not a police force,' Zeck cut him off.

The Lord Commander Militant reddened. He was not much younger than Heth had been, but he had come through his battlefields with little visible scarring. He was short, and his wiry physique appeared slight in his uniform. He was fighting the perception that he was a toy soldier. Zeck's correction did not help.

'If you'll excuse me,' Zeck said to the rest of the Twelve, 'I have work to do.' He strode away from the dais.

'How will you pacify the entire planet?' Ekharth called after him.

Zeck gave no sign he had heard.

Vangorich eyed the fuming Verreault, and felt the weight of his own helplessness. He'd spent months fighting to get the High Lords to act in time to staunch a lethal threat to the Imperium, and he had failed. The Officio Assassinorum had no forces to offer against an invasion of Terra. Was there anything left for him to try in the defence of the

Imperium? He could watch the deliberations. He could evaluate the efforts to fight the orks. He could, perhaps, just perhaps, head off more disastrous decisions.

Like you've been doing so well, he thought. How are you any better than these other fools?

For the moment, he had no answer for himself.

The fire raced to the tenement blocks. Walls impregnated by centuries of oil smoke and rotted by poverty ignited. Haas hesitated in her advance. Within seconds, her target became a wall of flame. Another variation joined the chorus of the great scream. The inhabitants shrieked, and were incinerated. The burn became a firestorm. It spread to the left and right along the Avenue of Martyrs. It leapt along the vaulting arches overhead and travelled on the backs of pilgrims, turning them into running torches. Soon, both sides of the Avenue were ablaze.

The Arbitrators stopped. Haas' plan disintegrated. The people tried to retreat from the flames, but the flames were everywhere, their crackle growing to a snapping roar, a wind with jaws. The pilgrims shrank from the heat and bunched towards the centre of the Avenue. They became a solid barrier of flesh. The crush was such that even those rendered unconscious by the shock mauls were held upright by the bodies around them.

'We're not going anywhere,' said Kord.

'Make a circle!' Haas called.

The Arbitrators moved into a tight formation. Their linked lockshields became a perimeter wall, a shelter against crowd and fire.

'We're too close,' Baskaline said.

It didn't matter that he was right, that the centre of the Avenue would be better.

'Can you move?' Haas asked him.

'No.'

'Then this is where we stand.'

The tenements disappeared in an explosive combustion. Haas sweated beneath her riot armour. The shields blocked the direct intensity of the flame, but the fire shone through the viewports of the lockshields with daylight brilliance. The thunder-roar of the fire was joined by the cracks of failing masonry and the crashing of collapsing wood. 'Here it comes!' Haas warned.

The near facade came down with avalanche fury. Portions of the building fell in on themselves. Other sections of the wall smashed onto the Avenue of Martyrs, crushing the pilgrims, making them into burned offerings. Haas and the other Arbitrators crouched, angling their shields into a protective roof. Blazing wreckage crashed against the ceramite. Haas crouched lower, absorbing the shock of the blows with her arms and legs. A heavy, burning hand tried to drive the Arbitrators into the pavement. They pushed back, shoving the rubble aside.

The roar of the fire had lessened. Through her viewport, Haas saw that the worst of the conflagration had been smothered by the collapse. Hundreds of pilgrims had been crushed. She had no idea how many thousands had died in the buildings themselves.

She could move forward now. There was shelter in the smoking ruin, the chance to regroup and return to the fray.

She clambered over some low heaps of rubble. The others followed, their armour protecting them from the guttering fires. The smoke choked the entire street and Haas coughed, wishing for a rebreather.

The suffocating air further smothered the flames of the panic. Many of the surviving pilgrims, bunched tightly in the street, were falling to their knees, retching. More powerful yet than the smoke was despair. It drained the urgency of terror from the crowd. It stole hope away and left the people motionless before their fate. On the other side of the street, the fire still towered from the tenement blocks. The collapse began there too.

Destruction marched up and down the Avenue of Martyrs, but in its wake, it left a kind of order.

Kord sounded like he was going to leave a lung on the pavement.

'We can't stay here,' he said.

'And go where?' Baskaline sounded no better.

Haas' vision swam. It was all she could do to remain upright. Baskaline was right, though. Any route they took would be back towards the fire. The space around the Arbitrators was fairly open. If they waited, the worst of the smoke would dissipate before too long.

'Our duty is not complete,' she reminded the others. Calm had been restored, for the moment. It fell to them to maintain it until they were ordered elsewhere.

Time passed. The air cleared enough that each breath Haas took felt like swallowing hot sand instead of burning coal. Kord looked up. There was nothing to see through the smoke. Even so, he stared as if he could see the object of his hatred.

'We need to bring the fight to the greenskins,' he said.

'We will,' Haas reassured him.

'I don't just mean the Navy and the Guard. I mean all of us.'

'Our oaths are different. We're called to serve here.'

'What good will that do? This could be our last stand. If we don't stop the orks, there will be no law to keep on Terra.'

'If the orks make landfall,' Haas countered, 'we'll be needed as never before.'

Kord had another coughing fit. 'Things have changed,' he said when he could speak again. 'Everything has changed.'

Haas shook her head and started forward to stand guard in the midst of the pilgrims, an unbending sign that the Emperor's law still prevailed. She would not swerve from her oath of office until death took her. It was her anchor, because Kord was right. Everything had changed.

And everything was ending.

The galaxy shook. From Segmentum Solar to Ultima, from Tempestus to Obscurus, the Beast unleashed its forces against the Imperium. Star fortresses appeared simultaneously in system after system. A predatory monster with uncountable millions of heads descended on the worlds of humanity. The fleets and armies of exultant savagery struck and struck and struck. The Imperium bled from a thousand wounds.

The worlds of Ultramar were spared the tectonic events of a star fortress extruding into near orbit. That was the only mercy. The first to be attacked were the agri worlds Tarentus and Quintarn. The skies over their cities turned black with ork drop-ships. Enemy cruisers devastated their orbital defences. Three companies of Ultramarines responded within hours, and they set the void on fire as a battle-barge and strike cruisers engaged the ork vessels.

Far to the galactic west, in the Segmentum Tempestus, the forge world Lankast convulsed. The geologic tides unleashed by the ork moon above it tore open vast chasms that traced jagged paths hundreds of kilometres long. Lava flows spread over the land. Entire hive cities were wiped away, hundreds of millions of lives vanishing into waves of molten rock. And in the more stable regions, on the high continental plateaus, surrounded by new seas of fire, Iron Father Bassan Terak shouted the hatred of the Red Talons. They met the ork siege of the colossal manufactoria with a rage that had its own volcanic force. Third Company's Predator tanks hit the ork ranks with the relentlessness of a mechanised, moving wall. The orks countered from orbit. Heedless of their own casualties, they hurled rocky masses to the surface. Meteor strikes pummelled the manufactoria and iron chimneys a hundred metres tall collapsed. The eruption of the furnaces was a solar flare. The Red Talons advanced still. They had no choice. There was nothing behind them now but flame.

But it was Klostra, a planetoid not much larger than the star fortress that closed in on it, that suffered the most important attack. The inhabitants of its colonies prepared for the invasion they knew they could not stop, the invasion whose blow would resonate as far as Terra.

TWO

Terra – the outer palaces

The sub-orbital took Wienand, Rendenstein and Krule as far as a nondescript Administratum region in the south-east sector of the Imperial Palace, half a hemisphere away from the centres of governance. Wienand trusted Krule's judgement in his choice of the flight. If he believed none of Veritus' agents were aboard, his track record suggested he was correct. The transport had the advantage of taking her in the general direction of her destination. She didn't tell Krule where she wanted to go, though. She didn't trust him that far.

The flight landed just as the moon appeared. The transport hub shook. Panic spread. Wienand transmuted the shock of the event into determination instead of despair. She and her escort managed to descend from the hub into the warrens of the underhive faster than the waves of terror. Deep below, where the star fortress could not be witnessed directly, the fear was attenuated. Once the tremors subsided, something like the desperation of normal life continued, though anxiety roiled the air.

In the warrens of the underhive, Wienand wished for something more lethal than her laspistol. Rendenstein and Krule were weapons in themselves. Wienand knew how to handle herself, but she was more dependent on the technology of death than the other two. After the assassination attempt against her on the Avenue of Martyrs, there had been no question of resupply. Anything taken from her quarters would put the lie to her apparent death. Rendenstein and Krule had moved the corpse of Aemelie, her body double, from her quarters to an alcove just off the Avenue, not far from the site of the skirmish. The intent was to make it seem that she had managed to drag herself that far after the battle. None of the assassins had survived, and there had been enough disorder for bystander accounts to be contradictory. Veritus would have good reason to believe she was dead. Aemelie's subdermal microbeacon implants would fool bioscans, whose readings would indicate Wienand's DNA. Only the examination of a physical sample would reveal the deception.

'Does Veritus use body doubles?' Rendenstein asked, the same thought occurring to her.

'If he doesn't, he's a fool.'

'He didn't strike me as one.'

'No.' Veritus would learn the truth, but not right away, and that was good enough. A temporary death, and the time to make her move, was all she asked.

They stopped at an intersection of passages. They were in a zone where the functional abutted the decrepit. The walkway mechanisms still worked. Conveyors of horizontal, interlocking iron bands, they clanked, rattled and

screeched as they hurried serfs along the kilometres to their
duties. The frescoes on the walls were black with grime.
Above and below was more of the tangle of mechanised
conduits. Tarps of varying size were suspended from the
girders, forming patchy ragged ceilings. They were rough
sleeping areas, the closest thing more than a few of the serfs
knew to a home, makeshift sleeping posts that were turning permanent for souls whose lives had become unending
drudgery broken only by the briefest rest periods. At least
they still had an official, if tenuous, existence from the
Administratum's perspective. Not much further down in
the underhive was the realm of the forgotten, where survival was so desperate a game that the line between human
and animal had been erased. Wienand planned a visit to
those depths. If he were looking for her, Veritus would find
her trail even more difficult to pick up down there.

'Which way?' Krule asked.

'South.' Wienand indicated the walkway.

'If you'll wait a moment, ma'am?'

She nodded, and he disappeared into the shuffling crowd,
scouting ahead.

'He must know you want to reach the Inquisitorial Fortress,' Rendenstein said.

'Of course he does. But knowing that and seeing its location are not the same thing.'

'What do you intend?'

'We'll have to lose him at some point.'

'Permanently?'

Wienand shook her head. She wasn't interested in test-
ing Rendenstein's killing prowess against Krule's. No matter

the outcome, Veritus would be the only winner of that battle. Krule had cost her a valued operative, but he had also saved her life. Her allies were in short supply. Vangorich was one she could count on with more certainty than her fellow inquisitors for the moment.

'If the opportunity arises to part with his company, we'll take it.'

'And if that moment doesn't come?'

'We'll deal with that when and if we have to.' She sighed, thinking of what she had seen in the sky. 'We're at a stage where having Krule in the heart of the Fortress wouldn't be the worst of all scenarios. We have to reach it.' Shoring up her political strength against Veritus was no longer the most important consideration. Nor was her survival. What mattered was the contingency that she could authorise. It was needed now. She cursed the High Lords for having let things reach this pass.

Krule returned after a few minutes. 'Looks clear,' he said.

They headed off down the walkway, moving as quickly as they could through the crowds, the floor carrying them on for several kilometres.

'It would be useful to know the extent of Veritus' control,' said Krule.

Wienand had been thinking that through. 'The attempt to kill me is actually a good sign.'

'You're still a threat,' Rendenstein said.

'Yes. If my influence had been neutralised, he wouldn't have bothered. I don't think Veritus likes needless internecine killing any more than I do.'

Krule's grin was not a reassuring one. 'So more attacks would be a good omen.'

'They would be delightful.'

At the next intersection, Wienand went right. An elevator platform large enough to hold a hundred at once took them down. At the third level, they got off, and she chose another walkway, still heading south. The crowds were thinner here. This route served fewer active centres. Krule offered to recon ahead again. 'No point,' Wienand told him. His earlier absence had given her the few minutes she'd wanted to speak alone with Rendenstein. 'If there's an ambush, we're better off together.'

The downside to taking the routes she knew was that they might also be familiar to other, hostile elements of the Inquisition. She couldn't lose herself forever in the mazes of the outer reaches of the Imperial Palace, and she couldn't hand over her agency to Krule. She might well not reach the southern ice cap in time as it was. Her best hope was to catch another sub-orbital from a point where Veritus wasn't looking. Another few hours of travel, if all went well, would take her to the next flight hub.

All did not go well. After ten minutes, the walkway they were on ground to a halt. The serfs using it groaned, then carried on trudging. A few hundred metres on, at the next junction, there was another mechanical conveyor moving at an uneven, jerking pace in about the same direction.

'That will do,' Wienand told the other two, and they took it.

The walkway passed almost immediately under a low, narrow arch. Krule and Rendenstein had to duck. On the other side they emerged in a long hall formed by rockcrete foundations on either side, and coming to a rounded vault a dozen metres overhead. There was a floor here, just below the level of the walkway. It was covered with the detritus of centuries, though at first glance, Wienand thought she was looking at a disused cemetery.

The space was filled with statuary. There were warriors and ecclesiarchs, Adeptus Astartes and High Lords of the past, and many imposing figures that likely had been intended to be the Emperor. None were complete. Many were unfinished, flawed material betraying the artists with splits and cracks. Others had been damaged beyond restoration. There was a vagueness to them all, whether their features had been destroyed or never set down. They were not gigantic. No single piece was so large that it could not have been transported by a group of unaided humans. Some of the chunks, though, were fragments of huge works. A finger two metres tall thrust from one heap, pointing at the walkway in accusation. A head as big as a man lay face-down on the dark floor.

Though the space had the shape of a building interior, it seemed to have come into being as a result of architectural happenstance, born of the juxtaposition of other structures. It had never had a purpose. It was a tunnel through which the walkway passed, and it had gradually accumulated the cast-off statuary. What must have begun as a random act had become a tradition, and then faded away. An air of abandonment hovered over the hall. The lumen strips were few and old. Many were missing. The lighting was deep night broken by weak pools of yellow.

'We're alone,' Krule said.

Wienand could see no serfs on the metal path before them. She looked back. No one had followed them onto the walkway.

'This is a disused conveyor,' she realised. 'It doesn't go anywhere still active.'

'Then why is it functional?' said Rendenstein.

'It shouldn't be.'

'It's for our benefit,' Krule said.

Of course. It would be nothing to stop a target's walkway, then activate one that no one other than the target would choose to take.

They'd found her.

Krule jumped over the walkway's right-hand railing. Wienand followed, with Rendenstein right behind. They landed between two piles of statues. Stern, unformed faces frowned and heroic limbs reached for nothing. The floor crackled with shards of ceramic and marble.

'Keep going,' said Krule.

Wienand moved on through the mounds of broken art. She looked back after a few steps. Krule had vanished.

'There.' Rendenstein pointed to a deeper patch of darkness in the wall. Another corridor. Wienand nodded and hurried forward. She didn't worry about making noises. Her enemies knew she was here. Just as they reached the passage, she heard the crunch of footsteps behind them.

Her anger at having fallen for the trap passed, replaced by cold venom.

What she and Rendenstein moved through now was not a true corridor. It was a narrow gap between facades. The rockcrete floor gave way to metal struts. Footing was treacherous. The light was even dimmer. The gaps between the struts grew wider. A slip meant a fall into blind depths. Wienand advanced another few steps, then stopped. The next gap was too wide to jump. She turned to face her enemy, laspistol in hand. Rendenstein moved to the other side of the passage. She balanced on the rusted struts, ready to leap.

In the gloom of the passage, the main hall looked brighter. Wienand saw the attack coming. The assassins knew they had her cornered. They had no need for stealth now.

There were five of them. They wore loose cameleoline robes. They would have been almost impossible to spot in the shadows and abandoned art. As they closed in, their camouflage covered them in shifting patches of dark and grey. When they were a few metres from the entrance to the passage, a statue came to life behind them. Krule had been more still and hidden yet. The two rearmost assassins, a man and a woman, jerked to a stop. Their heads snapped back, mouths open wide for air they would never draw again.

The other three hit the passage at a run. One turned as Krule drew his bloodied fists out of the upper spines of his victims. She laid down a suppressive burst of las-fire. The other two kept coming. One, she saw, was Audten van der Deckart. He fired his pistol and an expanding cloud of silver-white burst from its muzzle – a web, the protein filaments expanding to fill the passageway. The tangling, adhesive cloud slammed Rendenstein against the wall, covering her like a cocoon.

Wienand dropped low. The bottom edge of the cloud clipped her. She lost her footing and fell between the struts. She dropped into nothing, then jerked to a sudden halt as the webbing caught her left hand and welded it to the struts. The weight of her body pulled at the web, and the fibres began to cut through her flesh. She clung hard to the strut, trying to work with the web instead of against it. A constriction of pain and steel enveloped her arm.

She still held her pistol. She fired upwards and hit the legs of van der Deckart's companion. The man pitched forward. He reached for a strut and missed. His scream as he fell went on for a long time.

Van der Deckart leapt from footing to footing with a raptor's grace. He holstered his webber and pulled out a short-bladed power sword. He danced out of the way of Wienand's shots and raised the blade to bring it down on her head.

Rendenstein tore through the web. Her body was a dense crosshatching of lacerations. The web had sliced through her skin and subdermal armour, but her reinforced skeleton and musculature could punch through walls. Van der Deckart leapt out of the way of her lunge. She fell on all fours, limbs balancing on three different struts. Van der Deckart came back at her.

Behind, the las-fire ceased with the snap of a neck.

Van der Deckart swung his blade at Rendenstein's throat. She hunched lower even as she yanked on the strut in her right hand. It shot out of the wall and flew upward. The makeshift javelin struck van der Deckart through the chin and burst out the top of his skull. Rendenstein snatched the blade from his hand as the corpse toppled over and landed face-down above Wienand.

Wienand stared up at his features. Even in death, they were pursed. The meticulous discipline of his cropped beard and hair was spoiled by his flowing blood.

Krule was with them now. He tossed van der Deckart's corpse into the depths, then held Wienand's left arm while

Rendenstein used the power sword to cut through the webbing and free her. They hauled her up and headed back towards the walkway.

'So much for the story of my death,' Wienand said.

'It stood up long enough for us to get this far,' Rendenstein pointed out.

Krule asked, 'Did you recognise any of the attackers?'

'Yes,' said Wienand. 'Audten van der Deckart. One of Veritus' political allies. He must have relished the chance to put me in my place once and for all.'

'His presence might be another good sign,' said Rendenstein.

Wienand nodded. 'Veritus must have limited forces at his disposal.'

Krule held up a hand, listening. He lowered his voice and pointed back towards their point of entry into the hall. 'Not that limited. More coming.'

Wienand thought quickly. 'Can you take them?'

'Yes, ma'am.'

'Then you have my thanks.' To Rendenstein, she said, 'Let's go. No more delays.'

They ran parallel to the walkway, weaving their way past the heaps of marble bodies. Half-finished expressions of faith reached for them with judging hands and blurred shouts. Gunfire erupted behind them.

'He'll catch up,' Rendenstein said.

'Maybe he'll take the hint. And maybe we'll outpace him yet.'

They ran on through a forest of arms.

THREE

Klostra – Klostra Primus colony

They would hold out at Klostra Primus as long as they could. The orks had already smashed Secundus. Tertius had also fallen. There was no question that the orks would overrun this last outpost too. Gerron watched the great flood of orks rushing forward over the barren plain below the ramparts, and knew that he and his fellow mortals could not triumph. The war's outcome was a certainty, if the lords of Klostra did not intervene. They were coming, though. He had to believe in their arrival. To show any lack of effort in the defence would be unforgivable.

An ork star fortress filled the sky. It was as large as Klostra. Its mountains and valleys of iron formed the laughing face of an ork. Its tusks looked almost long enough to gouge the surface of the planetoid. The moon was an insult, a mockery of the principles upon which Klostra had been founded. From the vast maw at the centre of the face poured the ships that were bringing extermination to Gerron's home. On the flat, cracked, rocky vista before him, he saw nothing but orks as far as the horizon. And still the streaks of new launches came from the star fortress. The orks could not be stopped.

But he fought as if he could kill them all himself. At his sides, so did the other inhabitants of the Primus outpost. Las-fire from the high ramparts was so dense it became a blinding sheet of lethal energy. Gerron aimed and fired, aimed and fired. It took him several shots to down each ork. There was nothing wrong with his accuracy. It was simply that the greenskins refused to die. Gerron wished he could be marching against the foe. War on the defensive was disgusting. But there was nowhere to march.

It was the orks who were the ones on the move. They had no positions to take. They kept coming forward, always forward. Their losses were insignificant. And their return fire was even more blistering. It was lightning and hail, energy and projectile weapons. It was tearing apart the defenders of the wall. The ramparts were, for the moment, standing up to the assault. They were a jagged iron face thirty metres high. Their strength was the only reason the orks were not yet burning Klostra Primus to the ground.

'We're not making any difference.' Bernt, at Gerron's right shoulder, sounded like he was on the edge of panic.

Gerron didn't take his eyes off his targets. He shot until the rifle's energy pack was drained. He crouched behind the battlement to swap out packs.

'You'd better not be thinking about abandoning your post,' he said to Bernt.

'Of course not.' The other man's voice wasn't as strong as it should be, but he was still firing. 'But we can't win. What we're doing doesn't matter. The orks are going to kill us all.'

'We're doing what we have been commanded to do,' said Roth as she passed their position. She carried a sniper rifle, and was moving from point to point on the wall, taking down larger, more distant orks in an effort to destabilise the advance. She wasn't having any better luck than everyone else, but her other role was to exhort and threaten. 'Are you questioning our orders?'

'No.' Bernt didn't turn his head. In the darkness of the perpetual eclipse created by the ork moon, Gerron couldn't make out anyone's features. Even so, he heard Bernt turn pale at Roth's implication.

'Then shut up and kill more greenskins.' Roth drove her point home by raising her rifle to her eyes and dropping another enemy. 'Choose your targets!' she called out to all within earshot. 'Embody precision! Remember the example of our lords! Fight as they would!'

'Oh no,' Bernt said, so quietly that Gerron almost didn't hear him. He pulled the trigger, but he had raised his head above his barrel. He was looking at something in the distance.

Gerron popped his head over the top of the parapet. He resumed firing. He saw what had terrified Bernt. 'Tanks!' he shouted.

They formed a solid line across the entire horizon. Gerron couldn't make out any details beyond their monstrous size. The line flashed along its length as the cannons started firing, and shells arced through the dark. There was no precision to the bombardment. The orks had no need for that art. The shells landed short and far, blowing up scores of infantry in the plain, levelling the comfortless housing of

Klostra Primus. Some hit the wall. It trembled from the blows. The first real wounds appeared in its face.

The tanks rumbled across the plain. A black, greasy cloud rose in their wake. The roar of their engines rose over the battle like the voice of the star fortress itself. As they drew nearer, they became even more threatening. Their armour was massive and horned, designed for ramming. The cannons of their stacked turrets were gigantic. They were covered in secondary guns. Spiked cylinders rolled before them, already slicked with the paste of the orks who had not moved out of the way soon enough.

'How do we stop those with las?' Bernt demanded. 'We don't have enough rockets. Where are the lords?'

'They'll be here,' Roth told him. 'Now fight.'

'Why?'

She pulled a serrated whip from her belt and snapped a coil around his neck. She gave a yank. Bernt's head bounced down against the parapet of the wall. 'Our lords are coming!' Roth shouted. 'They will be with us. Now do them proud! Obey their commands! If you cannot destroy the tanks, hold them. Keep them from coming any closer until the great counter-attack is ready!'

Gerron had already joined in the fire on the heavy armour. Searing light erupted against the vehicles. Flights of rockets launched from the rampart. Clusters of missiles struck one tank at a time. A dozen direct hits managed to stop one of them. Its cannon fired just as it was damaged, and the top half of the Battlewagon vanished in the explosion. At the same time, the heavy stubber turrets raked the nearest ork ranks, punishing the ones who had begun scaling the wall.

The orks did not even slow. Their wave slammed against the wall. More ladders went up even as the tanks improved their accuracy and started punching deeper and more destructively into the facade.

We can't stop them, Gerron told himself. We just have to hold them, for a little while, that's all. He and the other mortals had not been abandoned or forgotten. They were acting as they had been ordered. *The lords are coming. The lords are coming.*

Kalkator circled the display table in the strategium. The weight of his boots echoed like the toll of an iron bell in the hard, open space of the chamber. The hololith showed the green stain of the orks spreading over the whole of Klostra. There was no clear point against which to push back. The orks had swarmed over the surface of the planet-oid before any adequate retaliatory force could be brought to bear. Kalkator and his brothers were outnumbered, out-planned, outmanoeuvred. Their base, a few kilometres from the front at Klostra Primus, built into the top of an isolated peak, could perhaps hold against the orks' full assault for as much as a day.

Kalkator had no intention of being run to ground. The advance would be stopped at Primus, and then the march against the orks would begin. It would not matter that the greenskins had no base planetside. Kalkator would advance until he had scraped the last of the orks beneath his boot heels.

He told himself this. He told his men the same thing. The real outcome predicted by the tactical situation was unspoken, though they talked around it.

'Any word from the Ostrom System?' he asked.

'None,' Varravo said. 'No communications since before the star fortress arrived.'

'But our vox is functional again.'

'It is. The problem isn't at our end.'

The implications were troubling. They were also nothing that could be dealt with now. What was relevant was that there would be no reinforcements arriving on Klostra in time to make any difference. 'Then this is where we stop the orks.'

'I don't like being forced into a defensive posture,' Caesax said.

'This is only a siege if we view it as one,' Kalkator told him. 'I'm not about to abandon doctrine. The strategic value of the colony's strongpoint hasn't changed. We use it for its purpose.' Besides, he thought, we have no choice.

Caesax nodded. He put on his helm. 'We are ready.'

'Guns in position,' Derruo said.

'Then it is time to announce our displeasure.'

Is this holding them? Gerron wondered. Are we holding them? Will our lords be pleased? He hoped the answers were yes. That would be the only victory he could claim. Nothing the defenders of Klostra Primus could do had slowed the orks. But the greenskins were not moving beyond the colony. They were using their strength to annihilate it. Yes, Gerron thought. Yes. We are holding them. For a few minutes. He prayed he would live long enough to see the arrival of the lords and their vengeance. That would be victory enough for him.

The tanks were close now, too close for their cannon fire

to miss. The wall shook with the unending barrage. The barrier still held, but it was deforming, weakening quickly. The fire from its battlements was becoming sporadic. While the tanks hurled their shells against the middle section of the wall, the ork infantry raised ladders on either flank, and the defensive fire now concentrated on repelling the climbing orks. Gerron was shooting into a rising swarm. The belief that he was doing anything to delay the inevitable was an illusion, but he clung to it.

Then, to the rear, booms in the distance. The voice of gods, raised in anger. Thunder and hatred from the skies, the whistling of incoming ordnance. Vengeance was here. Gerron allowed himself the luxury of looking up and back. He had an impression of clouds falling upon him with iron and flame. In the dark second before impact he had all the time in the world to realise that the bombardment was using the wall as the targeting point.

The shells hit. They were massive high-explosives. They were designed to shatter fortifications to dust, and with them any life in their vicinity. Gerron's world shrieked. It disintegrated beneath a blow too huge to process. He flew through battering immensity. There was no real any more. There was only destruction. He burned. He felt his bones pulped. And still he flew.

He landed. The blasts broke time into pieces. His awareness floated in and out, tugged between oblivion and pain. At some point, the bombardment ended. The roar of war barely diminished, but the ground stopped its eruption. As he lay on smoking rubble, Gerron's mortal agony granted him his wish. He witnessed the arrival.

There was nothing left of the wall. It had fallen on defenders and orks alike. In the near distance, the colony guttered red and black, its usefulness at an end. From beyond the wall, the orks bayed with the ecstasy of a war living up to expectations. Were there any fewer tanks? Gerron couldn't turn his head to see. He could still hear the engines, though. He could hear the eagerness of the green tide for more and greater conflict.

Marching through the wreckage of the colony came the lords of Klostra. Gerron began to weep before the majesty of strategy he had been blessed to experience. The orks had come to besiege, but the lords had denied them that pleasure. Klostra Primus was not a point to be preserved. It was a trap for the enemy. The orks had concentrated their strength here, and the fire had rained down upon them. Now the march of the lords began. Through his tears, Gerron beheld the unforgiving glory of the Iron Warriors heading his way.

The orks, unchastened, rushed over his body to greet them.

FOUR

Phall – orbital

The final wall has fallen.

After they were spoken, the words became a silence strong
as iron, heavy as death. It spread over the council hall of the
Abhorrence. It seemed to Koorland that he could sense the
silence spreading down all the corridors of the battle-barge.
It was the silence that followed the tolling of a funeral bell.
He had made real a defeat so great that for the Chapter
Masters before him, until this moment, it had been unimaginable. The fact that it had occurred opened the door to
other terrible possibilities.

The silence lasted for a full minute. The Black Templars,
the Crimson Fists, the Excoriators and the Fists Exemplar, represented in the persons of Bohemond, Quesadra,
Issachar and Thane, looked back at Koorland, and he did
not represent the Imperial Fists. He *was* the Imperial Fists.
He was alone. As the silence pressed down, dense with loss,
and Koorland saw the expressions of pity, horror and sorrow around the council table, his survival felt like a curse.

He existed to spread the word of an extermination more complete than even the worst atrocities of the Heresy. How did he imagine that he, an avatar of disaster, could pretend to have authority over the assembled Chapter Masters? Even Thane, so recently elevated to that rank, still commanded a powerful force. Koorland must appear to them as the voice of the abyss.

No, he told himself. Be the voice of experience, of necessity, of unity. Be anything less, and they will dismiss you.

Bohemond spoke first. 'Your loss, Second Captain Koorland, is beyond words. Nonetheless, please accept the profound sorrow of the Black Templars. We honour the victories and the sacrifices of your brothers.'

Koorland would have liked to receive the wish at face value. However, he had to take notice of the deliberate use of rank. Possibly a pre-emptive gesture designed to keep him in his place. If so, he would have to disappoint the Chapter Master.

'You have my thanks, Marshal. As do the rest of you, my brothers.' He meant what he said, but he was also choosing his phrasing with care, emphasising that he was among peers. He remained standing. 'Let me further express my thanks that you have all answered the call of the Last Wall. I sent out the signal because what befell the Imperial Fists must be our spur to action.'

'None of us needed that spur,' Bohemond said.

Koorland bowed his head. 'I did not mean to suggest that you did.'

'Then what did you mean to suggest?' Quesadra asked. His voice was calm, but the words were sharp. His gaze on Koorland was scouring.

'What has fallen must be rebuilt. Together we shall be the bricks of an even greater wall.'

'Which is to say...?'

'We must do more than act in concert. There have already been disasters thanks to inadequate communications. This must end.' All four of the Chapter Masters were nodding. 'It is therefore vital that our united efforts be coordinated by a single command.'

Another silence followed, this one coloured by surprise. Koorland remained standing a few more seconds. He tried to find a balance, conveying authority but not giving offence. Then he sat, and awaited the reaction. He did not yet have the measure of the warriors he was addressing. He suspected that he might find a sympathetic ear in Thane, who at least had experienced some parallel loss and sudden, unwanted elevation. Issachar was hard to read, though he gave no sign of actual hostility. Quesadra's gaze had grown even sharper. It now flicked between Koorland and Bohemond. The Black Templar's face had taken on a determined cast, as of one about to do battle. Behind the Chapter Masters, their honour guards were as motionless as ever, but the rising tension gave the air a brittle taste.

Quesadra said, 'You are proposing a step of very far-reaching implications. Some might see it as an attempt to recreate the Legion.'

'That is not my intent. There would be no change in banners or colours. We would be the individual fingers forming a single fist for the duration of the crisis.'

'History is rife with provisional measures that became permanent.'

'Brother,' Issachar said to Quesadra, 'do you seriously believe any of the men under your command would seek to surrender their identity as Crimson Fists?'

'No.'

'The same is true for the Excoriators.'

Koorland couldn't tell if Issachar was supporting his proposal or pointing out its unworkability.

Bohemond said, 'Second Captain Koorland is correct, though. The orks have the unity and direction that we lack. A divided Imperial response is doomed. We have too much evidence of that already.'

'And the Fists Exemplar,' said Thane, 'have direct experience of the virtues of combined efforts. Marshal Bohemond convinced me, I am happy to say, of the pointlessness of fighting alone, and in a lost cause.'

Koorland nodded. 'I wish we had had such a chance.'

'I'm not disputing the need for coordination,' Issachar said. 'I am questioning the viability of the second captain's proposed integration. If we are to have a single command, who will be that commander?'

The third silence. A short one. Koorland said nothing. He wondered if, when duty had called him to Terra, he had been contaminated by the political manoeuvring of the High Lords. He wanted to be direct. He wanted to state what was necessary. But his position was weak. He had to think tactically. He waited for Bohemond to speak first, as Koorland knew he would.

'The coordination of joint operations and the recall of crusades has been through the Black Templars,' Bohemond said. 'Continuity should be preserved.'

Quesadra eyed him. 'So the command will be yours.'

'Yes.' Bohemond was being as direct as Koorland could not be.

'I see.' Issachar was still carefully neutral. 'And what would your campaign plan be?'

'To take the war to the orks. We cannot think in terms of defending systems. We will attack the star fortresses, beginning with the nearest.'

'As simple as that?' Quesadra asked.

'There is no front,' said Thane.

'Exactly.' Bohemond continued to address them all, rather than answer Quesadra directly. 'The ork bases are appearing everywhere. They are not advancing along any discernible path. We cannot think in terms of blocking them. We must attack to eradicate.'

'You are proposing a crusade on a scale that we haven't seen in living memory.' Issachar sounded impressed.

'And what of Terra?' Thane asked. 'It is defenceless. There is no wall there any longer.'

'Admiral Lansung has been keeping his precious Navy out of harm's way. As much as I am disgusted by his actions in the Aspiria System, they have had the effect of preserving his strength. If Terra is attacked, there will be more than enough vessels readily at hand. Our move must be to await the arrival of our fleets, and then attack.'

'We will be abandoning countless systems to their fates.'

'Those losses are inevitable. Better to pull our forces from hopeless battles to forge them into a weapon that can actually win.'

Thane didn't look happy, but Koorland couldn't disagree

with the premises behind Bohemond's strategy. He thought Quesadra and Issachar were on board as well. The problem was that any unity between the Chapters Masters of the Crimson Fists and the Black Templars would be provisional. At the first opportunity, Quesadra would challenge Bohemond's command. There was accord on a single tactical decision, not on the larger question of leadership.

The discussion moved towards the finer issues of deployment and the choice of a target. The closest ork moon was in the Illuster System. Koorland took part in the discussion, but did not try to drag it back towards the crucial issue. Now was not the moment. There would be some time before the other ships arrived, time he could use to convince the Chapter Masters, his brothers, of the path that must be taken.

It wasn't the need for glory that pushed him. He was resigned to the fact that all glory for him was in the past. In the future lay only atonement and the struggle to keep the doom that had fallen upon the Imperial Fists from also striking down the Imperium. It was also more than his experience with the orks that urged his claim. Thane had at least as much direct contact with the enemy.

It was more, too, than the position of the Imperial Fists as foundational Chapter. The leadership of this crusade could not rest on something as intangible as a simple right of seniority. As he read the currents of power and rivalry in the council hall, he realised the vital uniqueness of his position. He was Chapter Master without a Chapter. There was no agenda for him to push, nothing to seek for his warriors. He could present a perfect disinterest. There would be no partiality to his decisions. The only dictates would be the needs of the campaign.

He would fight for what had to be. But for the moment, the terrain was not his to contest.

At the conclusion of the council, Castellan Clermont escorted him to his quarters. He did not stay in them long. He taught himself the layout of the *Abhorrence* and learned where the other delegations were stationed, and where the Black Templars had put Magos Biologis Phaeton Laurentis. He looked for encounters of opportunity.

He had one when he found Quesadra alone in an observation chamber. It was one of the smaller ones on the ship, constructed in the form of a chapel. Rows of iron pews sat before the stained glass viewport. Phall Primus dominated the perspective. The gas giant's bands of colour were filtered and changed by the tinting of the viewport. Above the frame was an inscription: The Galaxy Transformed by the Hand of the Emperor.

Quesadra stood close to the viewport. The tapestry of colours washed over the deep blue of his armour, and the bloody hue of his left gauntlet. He glanced over his shoulder at Koorland.

'Our brothers the Black Templars have taken to heart the full conception of a crusade,' he said.

The implied worship of the setting disturbed Koorland. 'Yes,' he said, noncommittal. He wasn't sure what Quesadra's views on the matter were, and a doctrinal dispute would serve no purpose. He joined the Crimson Fist at the viewport.

'You don't think Bohemond should be leading us,' Quesadra said.

'I don't.'

'And who would you prefer in his stead? Yourself?'

'It isn't a question of preference.'

'Oh? One of destiny, is it?'

'I didn't say that, either.'

'Do you deny it?'

Koorland chose his words with care. 'It doesn't matter whether it is destiny or chance that has placed me in this position. What is important is the position itself.'

'Is this what you intend to say to Marshal Bohemond? I doubt he'll be receptive.' Quesadra snorted. 'You might challenge him to a duel for the leadership, if you aren't too attached to your right arm. Issachar might have thoughts for you.'

Koorland wasn't amused by the reference to the Excoriator's bionic limb. 'If that is what it takes, I will.'

'You're serious.'

'The High Lords have failed the Imperium with their trivial, self-interested political struggles. I would like to believe that the Adeptus Astartes are better than that.'

Quesadra didn't answer at first. 'We should be,' he said at last, thoughtful.

Koorland left the conversation there. Not long after, word came of the Imperial Navy's victory at Port Sanctus. The news confirmed the soundness of Bohemond's proposed strategy. It also made the wait even more frustrating. But the other fleets weren't far. Then, even as the mustering of four Chapters began, the near space of Phall Primus filling with strike cruisers and battle-barges, came the cry from Terra.

The second meeting in the council hall was more solemn

than the first. Bohemond briefed the other Chapter Masters on everything that was known.

'The orks haven't attacked at last report,' he concluded.

'When they do,' Issachar said, 'there is no point pretending what the outcome will be, what with the bulk of the Navy still at Port Sanctus.'

'There are no forces close enough to help?' Thane asked.

'None,' said Bohemond. He tapped the data-slate on the table. 'For all we know, the attack has already begun.'

The worst truth, though unspoken, thundered. *Terra may already have fallen.*

Now, Koorland thought. He stood.

'Brothers,' he said, 'I wouldn't blame you if you regarded my arrival as an ill omen.' He paused, thinking of Lieutenant Greydove's religious awe. *The rest of the Chapter perished, but you survived,* he had said. *That makes you not remarkable but miraculous.* He did not share Greydove's belief. But he was duty-bound to accept that he was more than just a single Space Marine now. Being the last Imperial Fist made him a symbol, and one that had now taken on an even greater significance.

'We know better than that,' Thane said. 'You are not the cause of this catastrophe.'

'No,' Koorland said, 'but I can stand for it, and I will. The Imperial Fists do not exist outside of this chamber. The final wall has fallen, and now Terra is on the verge of falling too.' Then he chose to speak the obscene. 'Perhaps it has.' He paused again. 'But what I said a moment ago is a lie.

'How can it be? Because the Black Templars stand. The Crimson Fists stand. The Excoriators stand. The Fists

Exemplar stand. I stand. The sons of Dorn in their thousands are gathering to begin their greatest crusade since the Heresy. The Imperial Fists live on in me, in you, and in the war we are about to wage. If Terra falls, the Imperium must and will live on. We will avenge Terra. We will reclaim Terra, and annihilate every last xenos brute who has dared walk its surface.'

He beat his fist once against his breastplate. He had not yet sought to have any repairs done to the visible damage on his armour. He used its scars now. When the Successor Chapter Masters looked at him, they saw the worst thing that could happen, and they saw the survival beyond that worst thing. 'I said that we must form a single fist with which to strike the orks. So we shall. I will direct those blows. I claim this right not in my name, or by any personal authority, but in the name of Rogal Dorn, and in the name of the Seventh Legion, whose spirit we uphold in our every act and thought.'

He finished. He waited. Bohemond glared at him. The Marshal took a breath. He rose. Before he could speak, Thane stood also.

'Brother,' he said to Koorland. He walked around the table to stand before the Imperial Fist. 'Chapter Master.' He held out his hand. 'My captain.' He clasped forearms with Koorland. 'The Fists Exemplar will be honoured to follow you into combat.'

'Thank you, brother,' Koorland said.

'I see no fault in Chapter Master Koorland's logic,' Issachar said. The Excoriator didn't stand. He was watching Bohemond and Quesadra. 'The rights he speaks of are real. We are bound to acknowledge them. Besides,' he continued without taking his eyes off the two rivals, 'I can't believe that he would be unwilling to listen to sound military advice.'

'Of course not,' Koorland said. He wasn't sure if Issachar was completely convinced by his speech. His agreement might have been more pragmatic, a way of heading off conflict between the Black Templars and Crimson Fists.

Quesadra was impassive. His eyes were hooded. The gaze that pried all secrets from others now hid the thoughts of its owner. All he said was, 'Agreed.'

Are you siding with me, or sabotaging Bohemond? Koorland wondered. He pushed his concerns about motivation to the side. What mattered was the result.

Bohemond mustered a grim smile. 'I will not break the unanimity at this table,' he said. Then he too walked around to grasp Koorland's arm. 'Lead us well, brother,' he said.

The implied test was clear. If Koorland did poorly, what he had managed to create in the last few minutes would collapse. He accepted that condition. If he failed, he would deserve far worse.

But was there an undercurrent of hope in the Marshal's tone? Koorland thought there was. If he was right, then there would be real strength in the wall he was building.

What he couldn't know was whether there would still be anything left for the wall to defend.

FIVE

Terra – the Imperial Palace

The days passed. The orks did not come. The star fortress hung in the sky above the Imperial Palace with dreadful imminence. It refused to change its threat into action.

The orks hardly needed to bother invading, Vangorich thought as he walked towards the Great Chamber. The panic the moon's appearance had created had killed hundreds of thousands, and brush fires of frenzy continued to ignite despite Vernor Zeck's massive mobilisation of enforcers. Give us enough time, Vangorich wanted to tell the green-skins, and we'll do the job for you.

He had never felt more helpless. In the depths of sleepless nights, he faced the idea that, once the threat had arrived on Terra's doorstep, the Officio Assassinorum had become irrelevant. Why should he worry about influencing the political life of the Imperium or checking its excesses when there would soon no longer be any politics left?

He didn't like questions he could not answer. He would not stop fighting for the Imperium until he no longer drew breath. But all his struggles over the last months had been worse than useless. He had failed to forestall the crisis, and the crisis was on a scale he would have dismissed as laughable. He had been guilty of the same complacency as the rest of the vain puppets who called themselves the High Lords. His sins were, by some measure, even greater. He had been pleased to believe he knew better.

He'd been an arrogant fool. And now here he was, off to take his place like a good puppet on the stage for what might be the last performance before the curtain was brought down.

The uproar that greeted Vangorich as he entered the Great Chamber was tremendous. If this was indeed the final performance, it was going to be a spectacular one. The great scream had finally reached the ears of the High Lords. The Chamber was full for the first time in decades. In their tens of thousands, the lesser lords, petty governors and bureaucrats with leverage filled the tiers. They had come, ostensibly, for answers. But they weren't listening. Every voice was raised in argument, hurling questions, demands and meaningless threats. Some were weeping. Others had abandoned all pretence at dialogue and their shouts had become inarticulate howls. Vangorich walked the gold-inlaid marble avenue towards the dais. It was like making his way through the maw of a wounded, raging beast. The Chamber, to his grief, no longer held a government. He hoped that what replaced it was not the death cry of a civilisation.

A phalanx of Lucifer Blacks guarded the approach to the dais. On either side, the floor was a roiling ant hill of serfs and messengers. They rushed on errands whose meaning-lessness was disguised by urgency. Vangorich was surprised when Veritus' power-armoured form emerged from that press, brushing past the startled Blacks to walk by his side the rest of the way.

'There are less inconvenient ways of meeting,' Vangorich said.

'I had other business.' He gave Vangorich a hard look. The eyes in that aged, lined skull burned. 'You have been inter-fering in matters that don't concern you.'

'Have I?'

'I am doing you the rare courtesy of giving you a warning.'

Vangorich stopped walking. He was delighted to find that he could still laugh. 'Really? You're warning me. And here I was looking forward to a long and prosperous retirement, reading by the light of an ork star fortress. Anyway, I'm sure I don't know what you mean.'

'The Inquisition won't tolerate intrusions into its affairs.'

'You speak for the totality of the Inquisition, do you? And by the way, have you officially taken over as Inquisitorial Representative?'

Veritus glared.

Vangorich shook his head. 'Inquisitor, if you can't stay on top of your internal politics, I don't see how you can expect the rest of us to do so.' He started walking again.

Veritus strode beside him. 'I am trying to speak to you, Grand Master, because I know that you, at least, are not a fool.'

'I'm tempted to interpret that as meaning you do not have a high opinion of the High Lords.'

'I do not.'

'All such opinions may well be moot.' Vangorich wondered if he sounded as tired as he felt.

'I don't believe that. This obsession with the orks is a mistake.'

Vangorich kept his face straight. 'I can't imagine why the orks should be commanding so much of our attention,' he muttered.

They reached the dais. As they took their seats, Ekharth went through the motions of calling the session to order. There was too much uproar for anyone beyond the circle of chairs to hear him, but the sight of the debate beginning brought a measure of calm to the Great Chamber. Half a million people strained to listen. Vox-casters carried the debate to all corners of the vast space.

Vangorich gestured at the mass assembly. To Udo he said, 'I rejoice to see the Great Chamber so lively.'

'As do I, Grand Master.' The Lord Commander sounded quite genuine.

Vangorich swept his gaze over the Twelve. He judged that some of them, like Lansung, would have preferred the council to be private still. The High Admiral, in particular, was facing massive public humiliation. Others, Udo among them, apparently saw the involvement of the full Chamber as a way of spreading the blame for whatever happened next as widely as possible. The High Lords were behaving as if they were facing nothing worse than an especially acute political crisis, not extermination.

Then again, the orks had not attacked. Every other system where a star fortress had intruded would have long since been burning or enslaved.

The anomaly wasn't lost on the other Lords. 'Why haven't the greenskins invaded?' Ekharth asked Lansung.

The High Admiral shrugged. Defeat was corroding him further each day. 'I have no idea,' he said.

'Perhaps the Fabricator General can enlighten us,' Vangorich said.

'We have no satisfactory answer to give,' said Kubik. 'The behaviour is anomalous. One can construct scenarios wherein the means necessary to transport a body of that mass to the heart of the Imperium are such that the *Veridi giganticus* must rebuild energy stores prior to further action. But this is mere speculation, an inevitable result of our lack of data. Since this behaviour does not conform to any previously seen in the orks, the inevitable conclusion is that it is not simply their technology that is undergoing dramatic evolution. Perhaps even cladogenesis is possible. We can rule out nothing. The situation is an interesting one.'

'Does that mean there will be time for the fleet to return?' Ekharth's wistfulness was childlike. It was picked up by the assembly. The murmur of hope was loud as thunder, fragile as gossamer.

'Unknown.' Kubik's brief response was as close to a shrug as the Fabricator General came.

'The orks will let us know,' Lansung said.

The crowd rumble grew discontented.

'Is that what you propose?' Juskina Tull asked. 'That we wait to find out? That is not acceptable.'

'Do you see an alternative, Speaker?' Some of Lansung's old sneer came back.

'We take the fight to the orks.'

Now Lansung laughed. The sound was ugly with contempt and despair. 'But of course. How idiotic that no one else thought of that. I suppose you have a brilliant way of doing this in the absence of the Imperial Navy.'

'Yes.'

The one word shut down Lansung's response and brought everyone up short. The silence of a collective breath being held fell over the Great Chamber. Tull rose from her seat. As she began to speak, she walked along the perimeter of the dais. Her robes were a magisterial red and black. She orated with one bare arm outstretched and punctuating each point with sweeping gestures. She held her left arm across her waist, a fold of her robes draped over it, and she strode the stage of the assembly as if born for this moment.

'The defence of the Imperium,' she proclaimed, 'is not just the responsibility of the Navy, the Astra Militarum, or the Adeptus Astartes.' She paused. 'It is the responsibility of every citizen, of every human.' She tilted her head back, as if gazing onto distant battlefields. 'In this hour of greatest need, the Imperium calls upon all of us. I will not refuse to answer. Will any of you?'

She waited, and the cries of 'No!' came on cue, building on each other and on the anticipated salvation her confidence promised. Though he had no idea where Tull was going with this performance, Vangorich was impressed. Tull had always been a figure of great presence among the High Lords. The peace that had lured the Imperium into its deadly complacency had also denied Tull the opportunity to influence the currents of policy as much as she would have liked. Now she was in her glory.

'The greenskins have their moon. What are the numbers that threaten us?'

Kubik said, 'We have as yet no way of properly measuring the scale of–'

'What does it matter when we are billions?' Tull shouted to the tiers. Her voice rang with strength. It was the sound of defiance. Vangorich had a sudden image of countless iterations of Juskina Tull, stretching back through human history, standing on clifftops and hurling her indomitability at invaders, inspiring the armies behind her to the impossible. The power she had was magnificent. His concern was how she would choose to wield it.

'The orks have weapons,' Tull said. 'Don't we? They have ships. Don't we? They have the presumption to believe they can invade us? Then we shall invade them! We will flood them with such numbers that the fear they have visited upon our world will pale before their own terror!'

She took a step back, her face shining, as the crowd's roar swept over the dais in waves.

So much hope, Vangorich thought, and Tull hadn't offered a single concrete detail of her proposed miracle.

Lansung said, 'And how is this invasion going to take place without the presence of the Navy?'

Tull turned her smile on him, and it was eviscerating in its forbearance. 'We don't need the Navy.' She looked back to the assembly. 'We have the Merchant Fleets! We have ships beyond counting! Right here, at anchor over Terra and in the Sol System, we have more vessels than the orks could ever hope to defend against. I am issuing an immediate recall of all Merchant ships. We shall have a fleet that will fill the void. This fleet will carry our millions to the obscenity in our skies and destroy the orks utterly. This is the hour of the Proletarian Crusade!'

The clamour that greeted her pronouncement shook the walls of the Great Chamber. If sound could be harnessed as power, the ork moon would have been blasted in that moment. Vangorich saw one of Kubik's limbs twitch as the sudden peak in sound overwhelmed his sensory inputs.

When the crest of the celebration faded, Verreault spoke up, indignant. 'You speak as if Terra has no defenders.'

The smile Tull favoured him with was different from the one she had given Lansung. It was an invitation to join her in the light of victory. 'I am not forgetting the Imperial Guard, Lord Commander Militant,' she said. 'The Merchants' Armada will of course transport the full force of the Emperor's Fist. But we must strike with all the might and anger that Terra can muster. You would not deny the people this great chance to stand for the Imperium?'

'You know I wouldn't,' Verreault answered.

Vangorich was still trying to process the implications of Tull's plan. The scale of the madness was so vast, it outstripped horror.

Lansung was having some of the same difficulty.

'How are you going to destroy the fortress with unarmed vessels?' he asked.

'We aren't,' said Tull. 'As I said, this is an invasion.'

'Ground troops?' Vangorich said, aghast.

'Yes.' Orating again, she continued, 'I will not pretend that great sacrifices do not lie ahead, on Terra and above. Production will suffer. Those who remain will have to do the work of the millions at war. Many ships will be lost in the assault. Many warriors will be lost in the landing and in the storming of the fortress. But the orks cannot stop them all. We are too many.'

Warming to the idea and the role he would play in the triumph to come, Verreault said, 'Under the command of the Astra Militarum, the people of Terra will sweep the orks to oblivion.'

Lansung's jaw hung open for a moment. Then he sat back, defeated. Unless and until the Imperial Navy was able to aid Terra, he was an irrelevance, and he knew it.

'You surprise me,' Vangorich said to Verreault. The Lord Commander Militant was more of a political animal than his predecessor. Heth had always struck Vangorich as being more at home in combat than in governance. Verreault, though a veteran, had spent much of his career leading from the strategium table. It was easier for him to see troops as pieces in a game of regicide, and losses as statistics. Vangorich wondered if he realised that he was a junior partner in the alliance with Tull, as the Guard had been when Lansung's star had been in the ascendant. The plan was Tull's, as was the armada. Verreault's share of the glory would be what she permitted.

Vangorich caught himself. There would be no glory to partition. The proposal was mad. Even a group as prone to self-delusion as the High Lords couldn't be blind to that fact.

Yet Verreault was unfazed by his comment.

'Speaker Tull's argument has merit,' the Lord Commander Militant said. 'The regiments of the Astra Militarum stationed on Terra don't have the numbers we need against an entire world of orks, even with the reinforcement of the Penal Legions. The call has been sent to the entire Imperial Guard. But the Cadians, the Valhallans, the Mordians...'

'They still need to get here,' said Lansung.

'And they are already engaging the orks.'

Ekharth spoke up. 'The mechanics of recruitment will be complex. There is little time.'

'I have no doubt that the Administratum is up to the challenge,' said Tull.

'It is. This will be a mobilisation to give birth to legends!' The cheer that answered him wasn't as excited as the ones that Tull summoned, but it was the greatest Ekharth, a poor speaker, had ever received.

'When great sacrifice is called for, faith and inspiration are more vital than ever,' Mesring said.

'They are indeed,' said Tull.

Vangorich vowed to track down those responsible for giving the Ecclesiarch the antidote to the poison the Grand Master had introduced into his system. Now Mesring would be spreading the toxins of his influence even more effectively. Tull's strategy was lunatic, but it was also brilliant. At a stroke, she had Verreault, Ekharth and Mesring invested in the plan. Lansung was opposed, but he was a pariah. Udo was eager to distance himself from the High Admiral, so Vangorich expected him to side with Tull also. If Gibran, Sark and Anwar had reservations, they were not voicing them.

'The information such an invasion could gather would be invaluable,' Kubik said.

Even Zeck was nodding with approval. 'The people need

something concrete,' he said. 'The recruitment should redirect energy. Diminish the fear. Take the wind out of the riots.'

Then Tull spoke to Lansung, and cemented her pre-eminence. 'The Crusade will not be possible without the assistance of the Imperial Navy.'

'What?'

'The armaments of the Merchant Fleet are light at best. By numbers alone, I know we can overwhelm the ork defences. But with the *Autocephalax Eternal* leading the way, we will punch through with ease.'

Lansung stared at her with undisguised hatred. Vangorich would have applauded Tull's move if he hadn't been sure that she was leading them all to the slaughter. She had Lansung cornered. If he agreed with her plan, the Navy would be in a position that was even more subordinate to the Merchant Fleet than the Imperial Guard's. If he refused, he would be offering up the spectacle of the flagship remaining behind, the Navy sitting out a fight while the common citizens came forward at the hour of Terra's greatest need. He could not refuse.

'The *Autocephalax Eternal* will be at the forefront of this great endeavour,' Lansung said. Though he sounded sick, the Great Chamber resounded with more celebration.

We're doing it, Vangorich thought. We're doing the work of the orks for them. And we're cheering our own destruction.

'What if the invasion fails?' He heard himself making an effort he already knew was futile. 'What then? If the bulk of the Terran regiments of the Astra Militarum are lost in this venture, what defences will remain?'

'Your lack of faith troubles me, Grand Master,' Tull said.

'The Guard will return triumphant, and the orks will have been routed. There will be no need for defence.'

Do you really believe that? Vangorich wondered. Do you really think this fever dream will come to pass? Are you capable of seeing beyond the shift in the balance of power that you are orchestrating?

There were no answers. Whether Tull believed what she was saying or not no longer mattered. Vangorich could feel the machinery of the invasion already in motion. Tull had spoken, and conjured events into reality.

'This course of action is a folly,' Veritus said. 'This obsession with the orks will only open the way for the true enemy.'

His words were swallowed in the applause for Tull. The rest of the Twelve didn't acknowledge that he had spoken. Vangorich felt something that was not too distant from sympathy for the inquisitor. He might have Wienand on the defensive, but the man's hand was weak. Insisting that the orks were not the primary threat would make him appear delusional. Veritus was clearly intelligent and driven by belief rather than political gain, yet his dogmatism was causing its own damage.

When the assembly dissolved, it was in a spirit of jubilation as ferocious as the initial excitement that had greeted Lansung's victory. But there was an edge of hysteria, too. The hope was brittle. The investment in Tull's plan was total, but the need to believe in it was even stronger than the belief itself.

When Vangorich left the dais, Veritus walked with him. The inquisitor's style of interaction was as blunt as Wienand's was subtle.

'They are even greater fools than I supposed,' Veritus said.

'And?'

'The path we are on will lead to disaster.'

'The disaster is already here.'

'A worse one, then.'

'What would you recommend, Inquisitor Veritus? Do you see actions that either the Inquisition or the Officio could take that would alter the course that has been set? Would Speaker Tull's death matter now?' He didn't wait for an answer. 'No, it wouldn't.' Too many of the other High Lords were invested in the Crusade. If Tull fell, one of her colleagues would turn her into a martyr and become the new face of the endeavour. 'Or are you calling for the assassination of the entire Twelve? No, I don't think you are.'

In this moment, though, Vangorich felt the temptation of that idea. He walked faster, leaving the other old predator behind.

As he left the Great Chamber, Vangorich forced himself not to clench his fists in frustration. Once again, he had been helpless to prevent madness piled atop catastrophe. The closest thing he had to hope was the latest report from Krule. If the arrival of the moon had Wienand even more determined to reach the Inquisitorial Fortress, then perhaps there was something there that might be worthy of actual hope. He detested being in the dark, but Wienand, at least, was sane.

Where did that leave the Officio? At best, assisting an effort about which Vangorich knew nothing. The so-called Proletarian Crusade would march ahead, and the avalanche of events would continue. He stalked towards his quarters, filled with dread and wishing for the punishment of fools.

.

SIX

Terra – orbital

The *Militant Fire* was not a young ship. When Leander Narkissos had acquired her, five decades earlier, she had been showing her age. The Brutas-class cargo hauler had spent half a millennium making rimward runs, her fortunes declining with each successive owner. Narkissos' immediate predecessor had not, technically, been a pirate, but the dividing line had been a thin one, and he had finally been forced to divest himself of his business and his ship before the Adeptus Arbites seized both. Narkissos had been starting out then, his trade in goods transportation just showing promising growth, but he had been a long way from wealthy. He was able to acquire the *Fire* on very favourable terms. He had set about restoring her pride.

He was pleased to think that he had done well by his ship. Fifty years of work, of endlessly pouring his profits back into renovations and improvements, and it was really only now that he believed the *Militant Fire* was living up to her name. She was not a large transport, so Narkissos specialised in the delicate and the expensive. The ship's handsome lines and reborn lustre advertised his expertise. He fulfilled all promises, and as his reputation grew, it burnished the beauty of the *Fire* still further. Narkissos and his ship were an excellent team.

He was sorry that they were both going to die.

First Mate Demetria Kondos walked onto the bridge. Narkissos shook himself from his meditations on the coming end and rose from his command throne. Built into the bulkhead behind the throne was a small room that, with its book-lined walls, looked like a study, but was reserved for holding meetings with small numbers of privileged clients. Its ornamental status was also its vital function. It impressed the merchants he courted with its intimacy and sober elegance. It permitted quiet discussion in a location of high importance. It cemented deals. It served no command purpose on the *Fire*, yet it helped provide the means for the ship's existence.

It was also a good location for Narkissos to have a private word without having to leave the bridge. He nodded to Kondos and she joined him in the chamber.

'So?' he asked.

'The work is almost done. I won't say that it's doing much for morale.'

'I can imagine.' It wasn't doing much for his, either. He had ordered the stripping out of all specialised stasis fields and containers. The cargo hold of the *Militant Fire* was being turned back into a multi-levelled empty space. 'Can't be helped. We're going to be transporting personnel.'

'If we had time to do it right...'

'We don't.' The call from Terra had come while they were unloading at Mars. They had returned at full speed, reshaping the hold on the fly.

'She deserves better.' Kondos had an even longer history with the *Fire* than Narkissos. She had been part of the crew under the previous owner, and had been the lone member who had elected to stay on after the acquisition. Narkissos had been glad of her experience. It was colourful, and much of it not for official consumption. Narkissos cultivated a refined image, but trade in the Imperium could get rough. Kondos was good at spotting trouble before it happened, and just as good at dealing with it when it couldn't be avoided. In initial meetings with potential clients, Narkissos was the portrait of elegant discretion. She was the face of weathered maturity and relaxed experience. If nothing ruffled her, then nothing was wrong. Together they were the guarantee that the cargo would be handled with sensitivity and security.

'Yes, she does,' Narkissos said. 'But the treatment we're giving the ship isn't the big problem, is it?'

'No. Her death is.'

'And ours.'

Kondos shrugged. 'No, that isn't going over that well, either.'

'Captain,' Jasen Rallis called. 'We're reaching our designated position.'

'Thank you, helmsman.' He looked at Kondos. 'Here we are,' he said. 'Last port of call.'

'Last but one.'

He managed a grin. 'If we make it that far. And I don't

think the greenskins are going to be eager customers for our wares.'

They fell silent. The humour wasn't working for either of them. Narkissos had played the vox-casts of Juskina Tull's speech over the ship's speakers. He and all his crew had listened more than once. He understood the necessity of what was going to happen. But enthusiasm for the Proletarian Crusade had not yet taken hold of the men and women of the *Militant Fire*.

'What do you think?' he said. 'Is the plan mad or brilliant?'

'I don't know. Both maybe. I can imagine it working. If we throw enough ships at the orks, some of them have to get through.'

'Including ours?'

'Did you invest in void shields when I wasn't looking?'

'I wish I had.'

'Then, no.' Kondos wasn't joking now. 'We'll be among the first to go. We'll be the chaff for the ork defences.'

'I feel sorry for the troops we'll be carrying.'

'Captain,' Rallis said again.

'What is it?' Narkissos asked. He stepped out of the chamber, and saw the view from the forward oculus. 'Oh,' he said.

Behind him, he heard Kondos' intake of breath.

'I should address the crew,' Narkissos said. His throat was dry and his voice cracked. 'First Officer Kondos, please call all hands to muster on the observation deck.'

Kondos left without a word. Narkissos tore his eyes away from the oculus. He needed a few moments to marshal his thoughts without awe overwhelming his consciousness.

'You have the bridge, helmsman,' he said.

'Yes, captain.'

Narkissos looked at the rest of the bridge crew. 'I'll have the assembly piped in,' he said. 'You'll hear what is said.'

The observation deck was one level above the bridge. It too was ornamentation with purpose. It was constructed to dazzle. It was large enough to hold a thousand comfortably under a glass dome that rose from floor level. To stand there was to be surrounded by the void, and the sights could be overwhelming.

Today, they were. Narkissos paused on the staircase that spiralled up to the centre of the deck. He was taking in what might be his last few seconds of mundane reality. Soon there would be nothing but the extraordinary and the terrible.

He gave in to the trembling. He wouldn't have that luxury soon. His combat experience was limited to his time with the militia on Elysia, though the need for all ships to evade the system's pirates had taught him the miracles one could summon from a vessel. Kondos had served with the drop troops, so she would be ready for what was coming. Narkissos, though, was no soldier.

Yet he was going to war. He would have to muster the courage and dignity that came with the duty. But here, he was alone. He clutched the steel railing of the staircase to hold himself up. The fear took him. He wanted to weep. His breath came in hitching gasps, and he couldn't find enough air.

The bottom had dropped out of his stomach back on Mars when he had heard that the orks were on Terra's doorstep. The lurch had come again when the call to crusade had come. He had thought he understood what was coming. He'd been wrong. He'd been protected by a shield of abstraction. That was gone now. Above him was the reality of his fate.

It frightened him. He didn't know if he was up to the challenge of this immense day. Some of the shipmasters at Mars had decided they were not. They had tried to run. The Imperial Navy did not have the vessels to run them down, but the Martian orbital defences had executed summary judgements.

He heard the echo of boots against decking. His crew was approaching. He ran a hand over his forehead and through the grey waves of his hair. He steadied his breathing. He had a responsibility. He also felt, deep in his core, a stirring of excitement.

Can I do this after all?

He had no choice.

He cleared his throat. He straightened up. Then he walked up the staircase to take in the full sight of what lay beyond the dome.

He was still awed when the crew arrived. He could function, though. He stood at the bow end of the deck, and struggled to pay attention as the men and women of the *Militant Fire* gathered and were struck dumb by what they saw.

The *Fire* was surrounded by a spectacle of grandeur and horror. On all sides were the ships of the Merchants' Armada. Thousands of ships. Such numbers that they could have been called a swarm, but there were too many massive presences for so weak a word. There were ships of every size and grade. Private luxury lighters that couldn't carry more than a handful of passengers. Hulking Goliath-class factory ships whose retrofitting for their new purpose must have been a task worthy of song in itself. Mass conveyors a dozen kilometres long. Freight transports in such numbers that they were ranked in squadrons. There was so little space between the vessels that Narkissos could imagine hopping from one to the next. There was no room for error in the manoeuvring of the fleet and Narkissos felt his chest swell with pride at the skill of the pilots. The Imperial Navy could do no better.

He corrected himself. The Merchants *had* done better. They were here. The Navy was not.

Riding at high anchor, stationed far above the civilians, was the *Autocephalax Eternal*. It was almost as large as the biggest conveyors, a majestic cathedral of war. But it was isolated, separated from the others of its kind with the exception of a few escorts. The *Militant Fire* was in the midst of a vast concentration of allies.

So many ships. So much strength. Narkissos drank in the spectacle and thought, we *are* an armada.

And when he looked to port, he needed the strength of that thought. Terra's new moon hung in the void, waiting to swallow the Armada. Its maw gaped wide. There were no lights on its surface, no flights of enemy ships sallying forth. It was silent, inert as a skull, but as full of implication. When his eyes fell on the star fortress, the fleet lost substance. The thing should not be, and so it altered all existence with its obscene reality.

To his horror, Narkissos knew that this impression was not an illusion. Everything revolved around the moon, even Terra itself. The orks had become the centre of the Imperium. The magnificence of the Armada existed only because of the monstrousness it had been called to confront. Every act, every thought, every moment of what life remained to Narkissos was utterly determined by that inarticulate, unspeakable thing. Narkissos didn't have the words to describe what he felt before the sight of the moon. Yet it shaped his language. He, like every other soul in the Imperium, was caught in a gravitational field that reached across the galaxy.

There was no escape from the ork moon's pull. There was no shield from its presence. There were no walls behind which he could hide. They had all fallen.

The one act left, the one thing that kept alive at least the illusion of agency, was to charge at the horror. In that charge, he was becoming part of the new wall behind which the rest of Terra sheltered.

To attack the moon was to believe it could be destroyed, and without that belief, there was nothing. Narkissos understood the need for the Crusade now. He needed it even if he was superfluous. He was even more frightened than before. He was also more proud than he had ever been in his life.

He didn't say anything for a few minutes. He gave the crew time to see everything. There was no need to explain. Either they would know the same need, or they would not. When faces began to turn back to him, he said, 'So, this is what we have come to fight. We will be taking on troops, and we will be part of the great attack. Our goal will be to land our passengers on the surface of... of that.' He pointed without looking.

'Will we even get close?' one of the enginseers asked.

Narkissos smiled. 'What do you think?'

Kondos said, 'We've made difficult runs before. Been a few years, but it will come back to us.'

'Possibly,' said Narkissos. 'Or we could be blown apart in the first minutes. I'll say this. I don't see a choice. We attack, and likely we'll die. Or we don't attack, and we die when the orks sweep over us all. I know which end I prefer. If I'm going to die, I want to die a hero. The *Militant Fire* is part of the Proletarian Crusade until death or victory. I won't impose my choice on the rest of you, though. If anyone wants to run, go ahead. I don't know where you'll go, but I wouldn't have you at my side.'

No one moved. He hadn't expected they would. The silence that fell was one of unanimity.

Narkissos looked out at the Armada and the star fortress again. It was the most compelling sight he had ever witnessed, the most horrific and the most exhilarating. The emotion in his chest, too large to be articulated, emerged as a single, grieving laugh. Then he said, 'We're mad, aren't we? All of this is mad.'

'Completely,' Kondos agreed.

'Isn't it glorious?'

The crew's cheers filled the dome. Terrified joy reached out to the void.

SEVEN

Terra – the Imperial Palace

There were three of them in the Octagon. Veritus, Asp-
rion Machtannin and Namisi Najurita sat on the lowest
of the three tiers. For all the studied, wood-panelled
pseudo-intimacy of the space, Veritus was conscious of
how cavernous it was for such an encounter. Perceptions
were important. He needed Najurita's to be the correct
ones.

He had little choice about the meeting place, though. The
Octagon's security systems, whether sigil-based or technological, did not only shut down the possibility of attack in
the room. They also enforced privacy. The situation was
beyond delicate. The unfolding disaster was pushing Veritus towards a decision he did not want to make. If he could
avoid that contingency, he would. To that end, he sought
total control over the words that were spoken and the ears
that heard them.

'Where is Inquisitor Wienand?' Najurita asked.

'We don't know,' Machtannin said.

'Your answer tells me that you've lost track of her, meaning that you were hunting her.'

'She is a danger to the proper task of the Inquisition.'

'There was no consensus on that issue,' Najurita reminded him, 'never mind on the option of an assassination.'

'She is heading for the Inquisitorial Fortress,' Veritus put in. Time to calm the waters, if possible. He wanted an ally, not an enemy, in Najurita. She commanded a lot of respect within the Inquisition. Her opinion carried weight.

'And are you planning to ambush her there?'

'No.' Two failed attempts on her life. The chance of a quick and quiet elimination of Wienand's influence had vanished. To make matters worse, Veritus' forces looked incompetent. The very moves that were meant to consolidate his authority were undermining it. Najurita had been at least listening to his arguments before, and had been willing to concede the possibility that Wienand's relationship with the High Lords was a bit too comfortable. She had not signed off on anything more, and now, though Machtannin was stepping in to catch the blame for the botched operations, it was clear that her displeasure was primarily with Veritus.

She was not his only possible ally. He would act as he had to alone, if necessary. But he still hoped to avoid the more drastic measures. He hadn't given up on bringing Najurita around.

'We have friends in the Fortress,' he said. 'We aren't without influence there.'

'Inquisitor Wienand has more.'

'And if she carries the day, the consequences will be tragic.'

Najurita sighed. 'You do realise that an ork star fortress is in our skies? Your argument that the orks are not the principal threat isn't terribly convincing at this moment.'

'I'm not saying that the orks shouldn't be fought. Of course they are a danger. But the overcommitment of resources to this one endeavour will leave us vulnerable to a greater enemy.'

Najurita looked at Machtannin. 'You agree, I take it?'

He nodded. 'We can't afford to take our eyes off the moves of the Archenemy.'

'You know me,' Najurita said to Veritus. 'You know that I would never underestimate the threat of the Ruinous Powers. I am fully aware of what the Heresy cost the Imperium. But we triumphed over the Eye. Its activity has been minimal of late. And the orks are menacing us with imminent annihilation.'

'Which is exactly why all the attention given to them is such a mistake. Now is when the real enemy is most dangerous. The Imperium has been weakened, and is distracted. What better moment to strike?'

'That is a hypothetical. The ork attack is real.'

'What ork attack?' Veritus demanded. 'Nothing has happened since the moon's arrival. Where is the ork invasion?'

The look on Najurita's face told him all he needed to know. He hadn't convinced her of anything except perhaps that he was unbalanced. He was disappointed to see that doubt in her eyes. It was one he had seen many times before, one of the costs of the war that was his destiny to wage. One of the great strengths of the Ruinous Powers was their improbability. It was too easy to disbelieve in them, or in their danger, until it was too late. He had made that mistake in his youth.

He still bore the scars of that error. His power armour was his defence and it was his weapon, but it also gave mobility to a body that could no longer function outside of its ceramite shell.

He tried another tack. A last one. 'The fact remains that Inquisitor Wienand is a rogue player. She must be prevented from causing any further damage.'

'For all we know, within the next few days there will be very little left to damage. Unless Speaker Tull's crusade turns out to be the miracle she would have everyone believe it to be.'

'I share your doubts about the strategy,' Veritus said, and waited for Najurita to say something more. Her statement had bordered on the non sequitur.

Najurita stood. 'Then we are agreed.'

The meeting was over.

Machtannin and Veritus lingered after she left.

'What did that mean?' Machtannin asked.

'That she does not share our evaluation of Inquisitor Wienand.'

'She'll oppose us.'

'I don't think so. She's doubtful, but isn't going to throw her strength to one side or the other, at least for the moment.'

'Where does that leave us?'

'We have to try again.'

'Najurita won't appreciate being lied to.'

'I wasn't lying. She's forcing our hand. Wienand has too many friends in the Fortress. Once she's inside, I'm far from certain that we have the political strength to counter her moves.'

'A third attempt is going to be messy, whether or not it is successful.'

'Still better than the alternative. If she has her way, there may not be any turning back.'

'We still don't know what she plans.'

Veritus turned his head slowly. He gave the younger man his coldest stare. 'Your resolution is lacking too?'

Machtannin shook his head. 'You know it isn't.'

Veritus did not know this. At this moment, he had only Machtannin's reassurance. Veritus knew that there was no love lost between Machtannin and Wienand – what he was uncertain about was how fully Machtannin appreciated the threat of Chaos. Veritus respected the record of Machtannin's battles, but he didn't know the depths of his commitment now.

Veritus left the Octagon a few minutes later. He made his way towards his quarters along Proscription Way. It was one of the narrower arcades of the Imperial Palace, less than ten metres across. The vault was so high and the skylights so few and grimed by centuries of smog, that daylight never reached the floor. The passage was a land of perpetual evening. The lumen globes were spaced such that there was enough light to see by, but a walk along the Way was a journey through degrees of shadow. The flagstones of the floor were engraved with devotional sayings. The erosion of millions of footsteps had worn them away until they were patterns of faint lines, fragments of words and suggestions of meaning.

Thought was being erased from Proscription Way one

pedestrian at a time, but it was preserved and given rigour in the gothic honeycombs that lined the passage. The ground floors were emporiums selling prayer scrolls, altar icons and exegetical texts. The Way ran north-south, its gentle sinuosity carrying on for kilometres, its thousand merchants vying in solemn and twilit quiet for the attention of the faithful. Scholars lived above the vendors. They were the writers of tracts, the commentators of texts, the explorers of devotion. They laboured with the industry of obsession.

Veritus liked the character of Proscription Way. The scholars had only half the truth. There was no mention, in any of their texts, of the Ruinous Powers. But the faith they extolled was a necessary, if not sufficient, defence against them. The people who lived and worked here were fighting the war, even if they didn't realise it.

The las-fire came in a cluster of shots. The first seared his cheek. His instincts reacted before his conscious mind, reflexes taking over. He brought up his left arm to protect his head. The second shot creased his scalp. He lunged to one side of the arcade. The third shot burned down the side of his temple. Then he was against the wall, looking for the origins of the fire. There were too many windows, with too many people visible in silhouette. None were looking at him, none were armed. The sniper had stopped shooting.

Veritus waited, his laspistol drawn. Nothing. The nearby pedestrians had scattered, crouching in doorways or behind stalls. The sniper's aim had been excellent. His armour was untouched. His wounds throbbed and he smelt burned flesh. If he had been just a bit slower, if the sniper's first shot had not been spoiled by whatever random event had intervened...

No targets, no further attack. He started moving down the Way again, moving backwards until he went around a curve and the point of ambush was out of sight. He turned around and strode down the passage, monitoring all sides for threat. His temple throbbed with anger even more than it did from the wound. He was furious with humiliation. He had been turned into a figure of ridicule: power-armoured, but in full retreat. But he couldn't attack what he could not find. He hadn't even been able to gauge the angle of the shots. Even if he could level both sides of the Way, the assassin would be long gone.

He tried to think past the rage. The tactical situation had changed. He couldn't be sure that Wienand had instigated the attack but even if she hadn't, she had friends who dared act on her behalf. Who were they? Too many possibilities. His own position now looked more precarious. He reconsidered the deployment of his forces.

Vangorich let three hours go by before he ventured onto Proscription Way. He found Ferren Reach in a book-lined cell on the fourth floor. The sniper had put his rifle away and resumed his scholar's habit. Reach was the same age as Krule, but looked much older, even older than Vangorich. His face was a map of wrinkles deep as canyons. His hair and beard were lank, grey, and long. His stoop and his shuffle were convincing, but they were false. The body beneath the robes was supple wire, capable of remaining motionless yet alert for days. He squinted as if through cataracts.

He didn't break the act even before the Grand Master of the Officio. He was standing by the shelves set into the wall to the left of the door when Vangorich walked in. He looked up from the manuscript he was holding. He didn't look pleased. He nodded once, which was what passed for a salute from Reach.

'So?' Vangorich asked.

Reach looked back down at the book and turned the page over. 'First time I've shot to miss,' he said.

'You made it convincing, I'm sure.'

'He's counting his blessings.'

'Well done.'

'Feels like a loss. Don't like losses.'

Vangorich walked over to the Assassin. 'It's my hope that you killed an idea today.' He gestured at the rows of leather spines. 'That's a target you can appreciate, I would think.'

Reach snorted and closed the book. 'I wouldn't.' After a moment, conscious that he might be pushing too far, he added, 'Grand Master.'

Vangorich spread his hands, expressing regret. 'I'm sorry, Ferren. The dodge was necessary.'

'Why keep him alive? If he's worth attacking, he's worth killing.'

'He isn't worth a war. The balance is delicate. If we killed him, we could trigger a civil war in the Inquisition, or if and when they realised what we'd done, that would be just as bad. The agents of that institution, with Wienand in the ascendant, are the only useful allies we have right now. The goal today was to destabilise Veritus. Make him uncertain about his position and his attackers.'

Reach replaced his book. 'Well, job done, sir.' Somewhat mollified, he added, 'Think it helped?'

'I hope so.' Vangorich moved to the window and looked out. The traffic on Proscription Way flowed in both directions, untroubled by the earlier violence or by the unseen ork presence beyond the vault. This region of the Imperial Palace had been the least touched by the great panic. Instead of rioting, the inhabitants had withdrawn further into their hermetic studies. They poured their consciousness into the mysteries of faith, and denied the upheavals of the world. It was a nice strategy. Though not one, he thought, that the orks would respect, once they came.

And was the game he was playing against Veritus any more practical? He had to believe it was. He had to believe that Wienand was moving towards a viable strategy to combat the orks.

'Correct me if I'm wrong,' Reach said behind him, 'but we're putting a lot of faith into another party to solve the big problems.'

The irony made Vangorich grin. It was either that or curse. 'Exactly,' he said. 'We have to have faith.' Another hard lesson from the hard days.

EIGHT

Mars – the Noctis Labyrinth

Sklera Verreaux was the first to see a possibility in Eldon Urquidex. She observed the magos biologis alight from one of the *Subservius'* shuttles. He was part of a group of Mechanicus priests and monotask servitors. Draped in the shadows of her stealth suit, Verreaux watched the arrivals through a telescopic sight. Urquidex was speaking to the priest the Assassins had identified as Artisan Trajectorae Augus Van Auken. Urquidex was broader than his companion, to the point that he had a bodily presence unusual for the adepts of the Omnissiah. What caught her attention, though, was his manner of conversation. His right arm was up near his face, and his digitools extended and flexed to no visible purpose. Though the rest of his body had the same floating stillness typical of the Martian priests as he kept pace with Van Auken, the hand gesture looked a great deal like agitation.

When she passed on her observation to Clemetina Yendl, the Temple Vanus Assassin said, 'A magos who is upset could be very useful to us. We should cultivate his acquaintance.'

So Yendl did.

It wasn't difficult. Beneath her disguise of false augmentatia, she moved through the low-security zones of Mars easily enough. Urquidex was involved, as soon as he arrived, with the excavations beneath the Noctis Labyrinth, one of the veils Yendl's team needed to pierce. Yendl spoke to Urquidex for the first time when he put in an appearance outside the Labyrinth. She played a hunch. She introduced some flaws into her camouflage. Very small ones, visible only in close proximity. Just enough so only Urquidex would be able to catch them, but enough for him to realise she was not what she appeared to be. There was a risk. The team could afford her loss, she reasoned.

'Why are you speaking to me?' Urquidex asked.

'Because I think you would like to speak to me.'

There was a pause. The right arm raised again, the digits twitching with indecision. 'You are attempting to suborn me.'

'From a path you know to be false,' she said. 'It is the Fabricator General who is approaching treason.'

'I am alone with my doubts.'

'But you are being true to the Tenth Universal Law.'

'The soul is the conscience of sentience,' he recited.

'You are listening to your conscience. The Fabricator General is ready to abandon Terra. That is sentience without soul.'

One of the priest's telescopic eyes extended to examine Yendl, as if a study of her mask could reveal truths. 'How much do you know?'

'What the Fabricator General intends. Not what he can do.'

Urquidex's eye withdrew. There were clicks and electronic chirps as if the collective of components that his body had become were in debate with each other. He said, 'There is something that should be known.'

He incorporated Yendl into his complement of electro-priests and enginseers when he returned to the Noctis Labyrinth. The complex was an inverted hive city of laboratoria. The experimental centres functioned like the cells of an organism, at times working in isolation, at others linking with many in the service of larger projects. Urquidex's party descended through levels of catwalks and tunnels into a world pulsing with arcane energy and technological ferment. Yendl could not understand the import of most of what she saw. It was too fragmentary. Through doorways, she saw vast machines engaged in dances complex, massive and strange. The scale of the endeavours was too huge for any one consciousness to encompass, and she came to a greater understanding of why the worship of the Machine-God had such a hold on Mars. What was constructed here, what was brought to mechanical life, and what was unleashed were far beyond the human. The spark of the numinous crackled in the giant forges.

Though Yendl couldn't guess at the function of each piece of the puzzle that she witnessed, she had a sense of all the cells working in concert. A single project, perhaps the greatest undertaken, united the laboratoria. The cells were the mind of Mars, and it had but one goal.

Hundreds of levels down, at the end of a tunnel that twisted and spiralled and sprouted branches like ganglia, they reached the most gigantic nerve centre. It was bowl-shaped. Concentric circles of workstations and control thrones encircled a fifty-metre column of pict screens. Thousands of adepts were at work, mechadendrites plugging them into thrones and, Yendl guessed, to each other. The air was filled with the screech of binary cant.

Urquidex led his retinue to a post two-thirds of the way down the bowl. He settled into the throne, mechadendrites rising from it to sink into the base of his skull. Before him was a control surface stretching several metres in both directions. There were more ports and mechadendrites here too, enough for about half of Urquidex's subordinates. The rest turned to devices that Yendl knew were mechanisms of some kind, though so foreign to the ways of flesh with their clusters of rods and dials and energy discharges that to her eyes they resembled jointed metal sculpture more than any form of instrumentality.

'Bear witness to the Grand Experiment,' Urquidex told her.

She stood beside the throne. There were other attendants, up and down the bowl, who stood guardian beside their magi, on hand to assist but not assigned particular duties. Yendl adopted that role. She slowed her breathing. She achieved machinic inertness. She watched the screens on the column. They showed feeds from numerous locations. She studied them, but could glean nothing from them. They were fragments, glimpses of vast and powerful mechanisms. Other screens showed very little. In the corners of one frame Yendl recognised the dry docks of the Ring of Iron, but the imagers were centred on empty space. The remaining screens, easily a third of the total, showed Phobos. The image of the moon repeated at intervals along the height of the column, rendering it clearly visible to every tier.

For the best part of an hour, all that happened was a gradual increase in activity. The movements of the adepts became more frequent and faster, as if greater numbers of variables were demanding attention. The chitter and scrape of binary intensified. Yendl didn't move. She did as Urquidex had instructed. She waited to bear witness.

The event began. The energy in the laboratorium spiked. The machinery in some of the pict screens began to glow and spit arcs of lightning. The air vibrated with a subaudible hum. Yendl had the sense of being in a cathedral as a service moved towards its climax. Machinic prayer rose in a stuttering crescendo. Readouts climbed into red.

Then the vibration was not just in the air. It was in control surfaces, in the bodies of the adepts, in the floor, in the planet itself.

Phobos vanished.

The pict screens that looked at nothing flared. The image dissolved into static, returned, broke up, settled into a pulsing, jerking, tenuous existence. Tocsins sounded. More gauges red-shifted. In the centre of the frame, where there had been nothing, now there was Phobos, surrounded by a violet, violent corona.

A few seconds later, the ground shook. The earthquake lasted a few seconds. Its magnitude dropped off quickly until there was just the vibration again. Then that too stopped. The priests of Mars ceased all movement. It seemed to Yendl that they slumped with exhaustion, though there was no discernible change in their posture.

Urquidex said nothing to her then, nor during the four hours that followed as damage to the planet and machinery was assessed. Yendl remained as she was, processing what she had seen, assessing courses of action.

The Mechanicus had teleported Phobos. She deduced that the test had moved the moon from one side of Mars to the other. The game with gravitational forces struck her as reckless. The fact that the Fabricator General had ordered such a step taken implied that the risk was less than the alternative.

And the test had been successful, but Phobos was barely more than twenty-two kilometres in diameter. That was a long way from being Mars itself, and the distance it had travelled was slight. If Kubik intended to remove Mars from the orks' reach, he would have to be planning a jump hundreds of light years long, at the very least. Yendl would have liked to take comfort in that thought. She didn't dare.

After another six hours, Urquidex disengaged himself from the throne. Yendl, with the others in the retinue, followed him back up the sides of the laboratorium bowl. A few rows from the top, Urquidex turned down a row. Van Auken was waiting for him.

'Very satisfactory,' the artisan trajectorae said. 'Your conclusions?'

'There was a seventy-eight per cent survival rate for the sensors placed on the surface of Phobos. The same result for those in subterranean locations.'

'That too is satisfactory.'

'If these proportions hold for Mars itself, the twenty-two per cent loss will be reflected by over a billion deaths.'

'A regrettable but sustainable level of attrition. The Fabricator General's projections allowed for considerably more.'

'I can only speak for my domain–' Urquidex began.

Van Auken cut him off. 'Yet you propose to do otherwise.' The grating electronic voice had no inflection. There was no flesh visible beneath the tall priest's robes. His prosthetics long and multi-jointed, there was very little about him that resembled the human. Yet his puzzlement was clear. 'I hope you are not still intent on questioning the path the Fabricator General has mapped out. You will lead one to conclude you are suffering from apostatical delusions.'

'Merely a question of means. The arrival of the orks in the Sol System has created a new urgency, is that not so?'

'That is correct, on a number of fronts. The Imperial Senatorum is demanding the deployment of Titans.'

'Fabricator General Kubik has refused?'

'Of course he has. What sense would there be in departing the system while leaving behind major assets? Furthermore, they would be thrown away in the current tactic adopted by Terra.'

'How has the Fabricator General answered the demands?'

'By presenting practical obstacles. Explaining that the time and the means to transport the great weapons are lacking.'

Yendl realised that Urquidex was conducting the conversation for her benefit. She was amassing all the evidence Vangorich would need to prove Kubik's malfeasance. She worried about what courses of action might still be open.

Urquidex said, 'Is that wise? Moving Phobos to a different

position on its orbit is far from what will be required. Will we not need more time than we are likely to have at our disposal?'

'You are indeed mistaken to speculate outside your realm of expertise, magos biologis, and mistaken again in your assumption. The principles behind the teleportation technology have been confirmed. The Grand Experiment is a success. The work that remains is a matter of adjusting scale. A simple question of brute force.'

'I see.' Urquidex said nothing else, but did not take his leave.

Van Auken's lenses whirred, adjusting focus as he studied Urquidex. 'Your hesitation implies a lack of purpose or a state of confusion,' he said. 'You are creating the necessity of a further incident report.'

'The completion of this project will be regarded as nothing less than treason by the rest of the Imperium.'

'We act, as ever, in accordance with fealty to the Machine-God. Or are you saying that the preservation of Mars is unimportant?'

'Of course not.'

'The Imperium is more than Terra. We have already learned much from the rapid technological development of the *Veridi giganticus*. It is a significant probability that the benefits of what may yet be learned will offset losses incurred in the process. Study of the *Veridi* is more important than their neutralisation, especially if they are on the point of cladogenesis.' More adjustment of lenses. Yendl imagined Urquidex seen under extreme magnification. She wondered what psychological cues, imperceptible to the organic eye, Van Auken might be observing on his fellow magos. 'Or don't you agree?' Van Auken asked.

'I do not.'

'You are challenging the edicts of the Fabricator General?'

Yendl was sure she heard surprise in Van Auken's electronic tones.

'I disagree with their premises and their conclusions. But I will not disobey them.'

'You are risking much, magos biologis.'

'So is Fabricator General Kubik,' Urquidex said. 'It is the nature of the times.'

The conversation turned into an exchange of cant. As inhuman as the sounds were, as still as the two priests were, Yendl read an intensification of the conflict. Then Urquidex turned away, and started back up the ramp leading out of the bowl.

Urquidex said nothing on the journey back out of the Labyrinth. They emerged from a gate whose massive, sigil-inscribed iron doors parted just long enough to let them through and sealed with a metallic *boom* behind them. Urquidex chattered in cant to his retinue and his subordinates scattered on their appointed tasks, leaving Yendl.

'Have you understood?' he asked.

They kept their voices low, though that meant little in a society where augmetic hearing was the norm. Van Auken had accused Urquidex of taking risks. You have no idea how big they are, Yendl thought. She saw the delineations of heroism in Urquidex's quiet actions. 'I understand very well,' she said. 'Does the Fabricator General know how to stop the orks?'

'My data on that point is inconclusive.'

'But if he does, he has no interest in doing so.'

'Our knowledge base is growing exponentially. The *Veridi* are therefore an opportunity, not a disaster.'

Yendl suppressed a curse. 'The teleportation project must be halted,' she said.

'That is impossible, unless you have the means of an invasion at your disposal. Nor will I raise my hand in disobedience.'

'Then why show me all this?'

'So you can take the action necessary.'

'You just said the project can't be stopped.'

'It can be slowed.'

Yendl nodded. A delay would help. If it were long enough, Kubik might lose his window of opportunity. Circumstances and Vangorich might be able to intervene and force the Mechanicus to fulfil its duties to the Imperium. The hope was weak, and based on shifting ground, but it was Yendl's responsibility to grasp it. Shifting ground was both the terrain and the goal of the Assassin.

'If moving Mars is a question of power,' she reasoned, 'then an attack on the Grand Experiment's energy plant might result in a serious setback.'

'That is so,' Urquidex said. 'I will never cause it harm.'

'But if you were to be followed, without your knowledge, to its location...'

'That would be a singular and unforeseeable event.'

'We have need of many such events, magos,' Yendl told him. 'We have had enough of being their victims.'

NINE

Phall – orbital

Koorland was in his quarters, working on his armour. There were limits to what he could do on his own to repair the damage. Bohemond had placed the armoury and forge of the *Abhorrence* at his disposal, and Koorland would make use of them in due course. But the last Imperial Fist would first exhaust his skill alone. He could not wage war in isolation, but his acts as an individual mattered. So he would make his efforts at restoration count.

His seals of purity were gone. There was nothing to mark his history of battle except the damage itself. He had no wish to expunge all the scars. Doing so, he felt, would be to erase the final tangible memory of his brothers. It would be an act of denial. He was resolved to return to the battlefield with the price paid by the Imperial Fists visible to the foe. He would be announcing to the orks his survival, and the measure of what he would exact from them. The gold of the Chapter would shine again, but with the marks of its resurrection and the demands of vengeance.

He would permit no blemish to the crimson aquila of the breastplate, however, or to the badge on the left shoulder. The black fist would have none of its power diminished.

Koorland was oiling the aquila, seeing the edge and fury return to it in lustre, when Thane appeared at the doorway. Koorland looked up from his work. He saw the look on the Fist Exemplar's face. 'What is it?'

'An ork moon over Terra.'

Koorland had thought he had experienced the limit of defeat. He had believed that he had plumbed the depths of failure, and perhaps taken his first steps towards redemption. After the last meeting of the Successors' council, he had even allowed himself to feel hope for the first time since Ardamantua.

He'd been wrong. Thane's words were blows. The shame of failure clenched his left hand over the edge of the worktable and crushed the steel. An abyss rushed up to swallow him. He fought it back. 'What forces are there to mount a defence?' His voice was distant.

'Very few. The bulk of the Imperial Navy is still some time away.'

'And our brother Chapters?'

'No better. The greenskins have the sons of Guilliman tied down fighting them across Ultramar. The Blood Angels have destroyed another star fortress, but they are on the other side of the Imperium. The Space Wolves, the Salamanders, the Raven Guard... We have reports of massive engagements across the galaxy.'

'This is a plague.'

'Yes, it is,' Thane agreed. 'Three companies of the Iron

Hands are making for Terra, at least, though they have farther to go than we do.'

'Has the invasion of Terra begun?' Koorland asked.

'Not at last word, but contact has become sporadic, and this news is days old.'

'The latest information comes how long after the arrival of the planetoid?'

'Two days.'

That long with no attack from the orks? He shook off the stun and began to don his armour. 'Where is Marshal Bohemond?' he asked.

'On the bridge.'

'He's given orders that we make for Terra?'

'No.'

'What?'

Though Bohemond had accepted, for the moment, his right to lead the unified assault, Koorland found it out of character for the Marshal to defer to him to the extent of waiting for his command to begin the race to Terra. The only other explanation was unthinkable. He asked anyway. 'He doesn't plan to go?'

'No,' Thane said again.

Koorland strode to the doorway. Thane didn't move. 'Let me pass, brother,' Koorland said.

'Please listen to me first. I know what you're planning. That was my first instinct too. That doesn't mean it is the correct one.'

The last wall had fallen, and the enemy was storming the heart of the Imperium. The final Imperial Fist was alive to see the absolute failure of his Chapter's most sacred duty.

The ramparts that had withstood the Siege were dust. If he did not make all speed to Terra, he would be compounding shame.

'How can there be any question?' Koorland demanded.

'There is every question, if we apply the precepts of our Primarch.'

Koorland stared at Thane. He waited, balancing between rage and shock.

'What do we know of the tactical situation in the Sol System? Next to nothing. Force dispositions? Unknown. By the time we get there, we will be even more in the dark.'

'The Navy destroyed its target.'

'Which we might do, but the gathering of our strength, the gathering you brought into being, is incomplete. If you lead a partial force into a complex, obscure battlefield and are defeated, what then? When have the Imperial Fists ever acted rashly?'

'No amount of preparation helped us on Ardamantua.'

'Nor would it have helped any Chapter. What happened was a disaster, yet in surviving it, you can hold your head high. You are a symbol of resilience, not defeat. You came by your right to lead us not just through the Imperial Fists' foundational status. You earned it by coming through that defeat. Don't waste what you have won.'

'What I've won?' He couldn't find the words to express his disbelief.

'Think about what is coming together over Phall. Think of the size of the force that you will command. Think of how hard we will be able to strike the orks. If we do so properly. As Rogal Dorn has taught.'

Koorland unclenched his fists. 'Go on.'

'Even if we could reach Terra before the invasion began, which is unlikely, and even if we managed to destroy the ork base, winning a tactical victory, what of the larger strategic picture? How much good did the Imperial Navy's triumph do? One fortress is destroyed. The orks have many more. How many? Unknown. And they are deploying them at will throughout the Imperium.'

Each question was a challenge and a balm. Koorland needed the answers, and he had to think calmly if he was to find them. 'Thank you, brother,' he said. 'But if Terra falls...'

'I don't want to face that possibility any more than do you. But you are the answer. The Imperial Fists fell, but they live through you, and their defeat will be answered by a force unseen since the Heresy. If Terra falls, the Imperium will live on, because it must, and its vengeance will annihilate the orks forever.'

Koorland stared into the corridor beyond Thane's shoulder. He didn't see the walls of the *Abhorrence*. He envisaged the worst of realities. He pictured how he would have to respond to them. When he was ready, he focused his gaze on the Fist Exemplar again.

'You're right,' he said. 'We can't attack the planetoids one at a time. Our assault has to take out the heart of the greenskin campaign.' He almost added that doing so might be Terra's salvation. He stopped himself. Hope was forbidden. There could only be reality. 'We have to kill the Beast. And to do that, we have to find him.'

'Agreed.'

The impossibility of the task silenced them.

No, Koorland thought. Not impossible. 'We must ask different questions,' he said.

Now Thane stood aside. Koorland took him down to the end of the corridor to the quarters of Magos Biologis Laurentis. Where Koorland hadn't altered the spare surroundings of his cell, Laurentis had, at Bohemond's sufferance, turned his space into a small laboratorium. Koorland could see no order in the mass of cables, cogitators and data-slates, but Laurentis was thriving in his environment and rarely emerged from it. When the two Space Marines arrived he was turning his head back and forth between two data-slates. He was making entries on them simultaneously, the four digits of his mechanical claws tapping at their surfaces with the rhythm of falling rain. From his speaker grilles came a steady commentary that was more dialogue than monologue.

'Phylectic gradualism? Hardly. What are you thinking? Punctuated equilibrium, then? No better. Time span too brief, the result too massive. Oh, but you're assuming that the rules apply to *Veridi giganticus*. Why wouldn't they? They're still part of the materium. And they haven't changed into a new species, now have they? Haven't they?' He paused, considering his point, and noticed Koorland. His remaining eye twinkled. 'Ah, captain – I'm sorry, Chapter Master.' He corrected himself again. 'Chapter Masters.' The eye blinked. 'How can I help?'

'What progress have you been making on the orks?' Koorland asked.

'As subjects, they are fascinating and frustrating in equal measure. So much to speculate, but so few conclusions to make with any degree of certainty. We are being inundated with data, but all it does is create more questions. We are gathering more and more fragments of more and more picts, but never anything complete, if you follow.'

'Do you have any new conclusions?' said Thane.

'I can assure you, Chapter Masters, that the orks will surprise us again.'

'I think I might have guessed that.'

Koorland said, 'You know about the moon in the Sol System.'

'Yes, I do.' Laurentis' enthusiasm for his work, so strong that it was clear even through the artificial recreation of his voice, turned solemn.

'Why haven't they attacked yet?'

Laurentis' eye brightened. The enthusiasm returned with a vengeance.

'Exactly!' he said. 'That is exactly the question!' He snatched up one of the data-slates and tapped at it as he spoke. 'There are two primary categories of possibility. The first is that they cannot attack. There are numerous scenarios suggested by this hypothesis, most involving unprepared forces or a lack of energy, perhaps depleted in the journey.' He looked at the files he had called up on the data-slate. He shook his head. The reconstructed magos had so little of his original body remaining that the very human gesture looked odd. 'Most unsatisfactory. In every other instance of the intrusion into Imperial space by a star fortress, the assault has been immediate. The supposition that the *Veridi giganticus* could be unprepared to attack so vital a target defies reason.'

'And the second category?' Koorland asked.

'That they have chosen not to attack.'

Koorland exchanged a look with Thane. 'Orks refraining from battle?' he said to Laurentis. 'How is that more credible than an operational failure of some kind?'

'Failure would be a massive anomaly in this campaign. Unorthodox behaviour, conversely, is very much the norm.'

'The surprises you spoke of,' said Thane.

'Precisely.'

'But why would they choose not to attack?' Koorland wondered. 'What possible advantage would delay grant them?'

'There would appear to be none regarding immediate military concerns,' Laurentis said, 'but that is your specialism, not mine. However, if I may speculate...' He hesitated.

'Please do,' said Koorland.

Laurentis picked up the other data-slate. 'Examination of the effect of the moon's arrival is suggestive. Data from Terra is regrettably partial and it would be very helpful if it were more recent.' He looked up at the Space Marines in reproach, as if they were responsible for the inadequacy of his research material. 'However, we have evidence of large-scale panic. The military response to the star fortress also suggests political disarray and confusion.'

'I am not aware of any response at last word,' Thane said.

'No response is a response.' Laurentis replaced the data-slate.

Koorland felt the cold wind of dread blow through his soul. He thought he could see where Laurentis' reasoning was taking him. 'And you have a hypothesis,' he said.

'The orks are triggering disruption without having to

act. The longer they refrain from engaging in accepted ork behaviour, the more confusion they create.'

'You're saying that they're engaging in psychological warfare.'

'That is a theory I am considering, yes.'

In the silence that followed, Thane muttered, 'Throne.'

'How?' Koorland managed. Laurentis was proposing an unimaginable advance in greenskin strategy.

Laurentis gestured at his laboratorium. 'Answering that question is my current project. Fascinating work, Chapter Master. I have never had such an opportunity before. I am afraid that I can offer no answer that I find convincing.'

'Still less anything that would be reassuring, I suspect.'

'That is so.'

Koorland thanked him. He and Thane began to walk in the direction of the bridge.

'Do you think he's right?' the Fist Exemplar asked.

'Are you willing to act on the assumption that he's wrong?'

'No.'

'Nor am I.'

They walked in silence until they reached the bridge. The primary oculus showed the gathering of the Chapters' strength over Phall. The Crimson Fists battle-barge *Duty in Blood* and the Excoriators' ship *Resilience* had arrived. Quesadra and Issachar had rejoined their Chapters to oversee the disposition of their incoming forces. The Fists Exemplar had a small show of power to make, but the strike cruisers *Unwavering* and *Foundation's Dawn* were present. Several of the Black Templars crusade fleets had answered the call too, though the more distant ones were still awaited. The war machine that was forming around the *Abhorrence* could set entire systems ablaze.

Koorland barely glanced at the view.

Bohemond stood beside his command throne, speaking with Castellan Clermont. He gestured for Koorland and Thane to join him.

'There is something you should know,' Koorland said.

'You also,' said the Marshal. 'One of our crusades cannot immediately withdraw from its current engagement. Our brothers there have come by intelligence, however, that indicates we are not the only ones to come under ork attack.'

'The eldar?' Koorland asked.

'No. This crusade is operating at the fringes of the Maelstrom.'

'Throne,' Thane whispered again.

TEN

Terra – the Imperial Palace

'The Father of Mankind has been your shield and your sword for millennia. Will you show your gratitude? Will you stand for Holy Terra? Will you answer the call of the God-Emperor?' Ecclesiarch Mesring's voice rang out from the wall-mounted vox-speakers. His words were heard throughout the Imperial Palace. They had followed Galatea Haas everywhere for days now. Even in the Arbitrators' bunkhouse dormitoria, the recruitment call looped. She had barely slept since the crisis began. Now she was lucky if she managed to shut her eyes for more than an hour at a time.

When their shift ended, and they were back at the command post for the Cathedral of the Saviour Emperor precinct, Ottmar Kord asked her, 'Are you coming?'

'Where?' She was sitting on her bunk and had just stored her equipment in her footlocker. The other two were still kitted out.

'To the recruitment field. We are.' He indicated Baskaline and himself.

'Both of you?'

'Most of the station, I think.'

She'd heard the talk. 'You're all really going through with it?'

Kord looked baffled. 'Of course we are. Why did you think we wouldn't?'

'Because we are sworn to the Adeptus Arbites, not the Astra Militarum.'

'You can't mean that.'

Now it was her turn to be confused. 'Why not?'

'You don't intend to answer the call?'

'It isn't for us.'

'Isn't it? Then why do we hear it?'

'It's being played across Terra, Ottmar. There are no exceptions being made.'

'Exactly.'

She shook her head. 'We're needed here.' Why couldn't he see that?

Kord looked disappointed. 'I never thought you would be the one to lack faith.'

She stood up and stepped into his personal space. They were the same height. Her face was centimetres from his. 'I won't allow you to question my devotion to the Emperor.'

'Then why...?' Kord began.

'My duty is here. So is yours. Will you leave Terra defenceless?'

'Listen to yourself. Our duty is to defend the Imperial Law, not Terra.'

'What I meant–'

Baskaline didn't let her finish. 'I think you spoke with your heart,' he said.

She hesitated.

Kord said, 'If Terra falls, there will be no law to uphold.'

Still she said nothing. She wasn't sure if she wanted to convince Kord or have him convince her.

'At least come with us and see,' he urged. 'Decide then.'

What harm in that? she wondered.

'The Emperor sees into your soul,' Mesring's voice proclaimed from the dormitorium speaker. 'He knows the truth of your devotion. But do you? Prove it to yourself. Know that you are worthy of joining the ranks of the saints. Lord or serf, we are summoned one and all. There is only duty. There is only one answer.'

'All right,' Haas told Kord.

'Bring your armour and weapons,' Kord said.

'Why? Are we expecting trouble?'

'No.' His eyes shone. 'Victory.'

The Clanium Library looked much as it had before the Battle of Port Sanctus. The maps, the chronometric displays and quasi-spatial projector still sat on the shelves. The paraphernalia of Lansung's theatre hadn't been removed. But the displays were inert. The library was derelict. A veneer of defeat, as tangible as dust, as cold as wax, had settled over the space. It even coated the man who leaned over the dark hololithic table. He held a bottle of amasec in one hand. Two more lay empty on the floor.

Lansung didn't look up when Vangorich approached. 'What do you want?' he said.

The High Admiral slurred, but Vangorich doubted he was as drunk as he'd hoped to be by this point.

'I want your help,' the Grand Master said.

Lansung snorted. He took a drink from the bottle. It clunked hard against the table surface when he brought it back down. 'Then you're in an even sorrier state than I am. My condolences.'

Vangorich ignored the self-pity. 'We know what we think of each other,' he said.

Lansung toasted that with another swig. 'That we do.'

'Then you know that I've never doubted your skills in battle.'

'Flatterer.'

'So why are you being an idiot?'

Lansung finally looked up.

'What do you think of Tull's crusade?' Vangorich asked.

'It's doomed.'

'So why lead it? I never tagged you as suicidal.'

'No choice,' Lansung said. 'If I don't lead the fleet, I'm a coward.'

'So?'

'So?'

'If the effort is doomed, what does it matter to you that you're saving face? You'll be dead.'

'What are you saying?'

'That you must stay. If Tull's scheme fails, Terra will need something to hold the orks back until help arrives.'

'You're putting a lot of faith in a single flagship and her escorts.'

'And her commander.'

Lansung looked thoughtful. He didn't drink. 'And if the Proletarian Crusade fails because the *Autocephalax Eternal* left the civilian fleet to be slaughtered?'

'With the number of ships involved, how much of a difference would the *Autocephalax* make?'

Lansung shrugged. 'Some.' He frowned. Vangorich watched him work out the vectors of the coming void war. 'In the end,' he said, 'the fleet will get through or it won't regardless of the Navy's assistance.'

'Then hold back. Live a bit longer.'

Eyes exhausted by failure, Lansung said, 'And can I quote you, Grand Master, as having urged my cowardice?'

'You mean your sanity.'

The Fields of Winged Victory had not been true fields for over fifteen hundred years. The last trace of greenery had burned during the Siege, and the area had been paved over with rockcrete during the reconstruction. The name retained some justification in the fact that this was one of the few large spaces of the Imperial Palace that was open to the sky. It covered over a thousand hectares, and its normal use was as one of the great parade and exercise grounds for Terra's regiments of the Astra Militarum. Though the material of its surface was utilitarian, it was painted with giant reproductions of the regimental arms. It took a company's worth of artisan serfs to keep the heraldry in good repair.

The Fields were lower than the surrounding regions of the Palace. As they walked down the Boulevard of the Militant Witness, Haas had a good perspective of the activity. The preparations for the myth the Proletarian Crusade would surely become were a wonder in their own right. The volunteers were pouring in by the thousands along roads feeding into the southern third of the Fields. Along the periphery, Administratum officers channelled the arrivals towards the hundreds of registration stations. The ranks of the stations took up the middle third of the Fields. From there, the recruits moved towards mustering points in the north section where shuttles took them off to the starports. Thence, they would be transported to the waiting ships in orbit.

Haas paused at the top of the descent. Awe robbed her of movement and breath. From this vantage point, she saw the shaping of a confused flood into ordered geometry. She was looking at a great army in the process of creation. Out of the street crowd came phalanx upon phalanx, each a thousand strong. She knew that most of the people below had never held a weapon, unless they had emerged from the underhives, for Mesring's voice had reached there too. These were civilians, not soldiers. They had no training, nor would they receive any. There was no time. And yet, as the phalanxes moved turn by turn to the shuttles, the vision was one of military precision, of the individual transformed into a sublime war machine. The people were nothing as simple as cogs. Their incorporation into the greater being was at a much more intimate, more elementary level. Cogs were still components. Here, at the end of the process, the individual had ceased to be, its existence making way for a new, larger whole. A molecular alchemy.

Haas started walking again. She caught up to Kord. Stunned, he had slowed to a stumble. They had lost Baskaline in the flow of the crowd.

'When is the embarkation?' Haas asked.

'It's happening now. The Armada is launching tomorrow.'

I just came to see, Haas told herself. I just came to see. The refrain was weak. Even stronger than the physical current was the rush of purpose.

For the first time in days, Haas no longer heard Mesring's summons. Another voice spoke to the assembled volunteers. Massive pict screens, fifty metres on a side, rose above the edge of the Fields at regular intervals. They all showed the same recording. Juskina Tull towered over the recruits in all her magnificence. Mesring was the voice of the call, but hers was the voice, and hers was the face, of the Crusade itself. It was her vision that had been given material form. She wore robes of purest black, and a diagonal sash of deep crimson. She gave the impression of being in uniform, though the design did not belong to any regiment. She was regal, yet humbled by the people who were making her plan come to pass. She was imperious, her profile cold in its perfection. In her bearing, she was a colossus, presiding over the shifting formations of insects below. Her voice was the ringing iron of command. But in her words, she was welcoming, she was warmth, she was the delight of triumph.

'Warriors of the Proletarian Crusade, I thank you for the struggle you are about to wage.' She paused. Her smile became ferocious. 'I thank you for the victory to come!'

The Fields of Winged Victory echoed with the roar. Haas had faced the great scream of the masses when the orks had arrived. Now she was swept up by their desperate challenge to the enemy. There was an edge of hysteria to the joy, but it was real all the same, and Haas joined in.

She and Kord were now a few steps away from the Administratum officials controlling the flow at the end of their street.

In the recording, the Speaker for the Chartist Captains paused, her smile becoming almost gentle. The illusion was perfect. It seemed to Haas that Tull really saw the masses, and listened to their cry, and waited for the people to have their moment. Then she spoke again.

'You are not trained soldiers. But you are warriors. The ships that you will board are not warships. But they will wage war. And know that you will have at your side the strength of the Imperial Guard.' She turned her head, as if focusing on a different group in the grounds below her projection. 'Let yourselves be heard, heroes of the Astra Militarum! Granite Myrmidons! Auroran Rifles! Jupiter Storm! Eagles of Nazca! Orion Watch!'

As each regiment was called, another roar went up, from different regions of the Fields. The bulk of the Astra Militarum contingents were not mustering here. They were being transported directly from their barracks to the Armada. But entire companies from all of them were present. They were being attached to the civilian formations to give them direction and boost their bravado even more.

Haas understood the purpose behind the integration. She could see how perfectly orchestrated the operation was. And she found it very hard to care, because it was all necessary. If the Proletarian Crusade was to be successful, the participation had to be massive.

And it had to succeed, she thought. The consequences of failure were so dark that she couldn't consider them. No one of faith would dare.

She barely noticed that they had passed the Administratum checkpoint and been channelled towards a registration station three rows up and ten aisles over. The queue was long but moved steadily. Haas couldn't take her eyes off Tull, couldn't turn away from the message being vox-cast across the Fields of Winged Victory. She had difficulty remembering why she had come here in the first place. To observe? Really? What was she thinking?

What sort of faithless coward came to observe the heroes and martyrs, and then walked away?

She brought her hand to her belt. She tapped the handle of her shock maul. More than a weapon, it was her staff of office. It represented the task to which she had devoted her life. She had to be sure that she was not abandoning her duty for the sake of selfish adventure. She closed her eyes for a moment. She could still hear Tull's speech, which had looped back to praise of the Chartist Captains. She was shielded, though, from the sight of the Speaker's overwhelming charisma.

She knew what she wanted to do. She had to know that it was the right thing to do.

Movement ahead of her. Kord walking forward. Eyes still closed, she took another step. Still thinking.

'You're coming. You know you are,' Kord said.

She kept her eyes shut. 'I don't know. I refuse to be derelict.'

'When have I ever been?'

'Never,' she admitted.

'I'm going because I...' His voice trailed off.

A hush falling on all sides. Like a cold wind blowing over

the Fields of Winged Victory. Tull's voice carrying on, but sounding less convincing without the answering shouts. Sounding hollow.

Tull opened her eyes. Everyone was looking up. The blood had drained from Kord's face. So had the fire in his eyes.

The ork moon had risen.

The sky over the Fields had no obstructions. There were very few other locations in the Imperial Palace where so much of the firmament was visible, on those rare occasions that the smog of Terra cleared away. This evening, the stars were out.

They were eclipsed by the fortress. It rode the heavens with brute arrogance, and made a mockery of the Emperor's sacred home. Haas stared at the planetoid. Her heart swelled with a pure, sanctifying hatred.

She had her answer. She was going. She would tear the laughter from the throats of the orks. Even if she had to do it herself, she would bring darkness to that accursed moon.

ELEVEN

Terra – the Imperial Palace

They stood on the second cloister level of the Daylight Wall. Below them was the entrance to the chapel ordinary. The spaces between the columns were narrow, the vaults themselves masked by stained glass. Concealment was easy. The view below was clear.

'Every day?' Machtannin said.

'We haven't had long enough to tell if this is a habit of long standing. But since we began observations, yes.'

Machtannin looked to the west, to the corner and the northward arm of the cloister. The lower colonnade had wider spaces. The walk from the chapel ordinary to the Great Chamber would take the target down that route. Machtannin would have several brief opportunities for a shot. One would be enough.

There was some pedestrian traffic in the cloister's lower level. Enough for witnesses, not enough for a hindrance. The upper gallery was deserted. No one had gone through in the last twenty-four hours, and Veritus had ensured privacy by locking the doors at both ends. Good.

'Well?' Veritus asked.

Machtannin nodded. 'Making the kill and retreating should be simple enough.' He stepped away from the vault, into the deeper shadows of the gallery's exterior wall. 'So we're doing this.'

'We don't have the luxury of prevarication,' Veritus said. 'Time is limited and precious.'

'But you aren't sure he was behind the attempt on your life. That might have been Wienand's move.'

'I'm aware of that. I know this is not ideal. But it must be done. Assume that Grand Master Vangorich is not responsible for the attempt. He and Wienand are allies. That much is clear.'

'Even so, the repercussions...'

'We can weather them.'

'Are we that sure of our positions?'

'Not as sure as I would like to be,' Veritus admitted. 'But Vangorich is too dangerous. He is undisputed as Grand Master. The Officio Assassinorum has a unity of leadership and purpose that makes it too grave a threat to ignore. Decapitated, it will stagger before finding a new leader, and there may be internal strife.'

'Making it easier to control.'

'Exactly.'

Machtannin sighed.

'Do you know,' he said, 'there are times when it seems we are doing the work of the Ruinous Powers for them.'

Veritus closed on the younger man. The bulk of his power

armour cast the other inquisitor into deeper shadow. 'You will never utter those words again,' he hissed.

Machtannin tensed. Veritus waited. They both knew there would be no violence here. Not because they must not draw attention to their location. Not because Veritus had the arsenal to overcome Machtannin's greater speed. But because of the power of Veritus' moral authority. And because their calling was too important.

'Apologies,' Machtannin said. 'I won't forget myself again.'

Veritus stepped back, satisfied. 'I wish for a more straightforward path too,' he said. 'But remember that we have the purity of true purpose.'

Machtannin nodded. 'I do.'

'Good.' He glanced back in the direction of the north cloister. 'Make sure there are witnesses,' he said, 'and shoot when I'm walking with him. We need that doubt about whether he was the target.' That was why he had insisted Machtannin use a sniper rifle. The attack had to look like a second attempt on his life.

'In other words, you want me to miss.'

'See that you don't.'

He stopped at the chapel. He maintained the practice, forced to keep going through the steps of a pointless dance. The High Lords still had him watched, he was sure, if only as a matter of course. He doubted they were interested in the reports. Not now. There was only the Proletarian Crusade now, and the hopes that went with it. Juskina Tull had most of her peers so invested in her scheme, they needed it to work as badly as she did.

We all need it to work, Vangorich thought. Even those who don't believe it will.

He performed his theatre of worship, and reflected on how badly he had failed the true object of his devotion. He mouthed what observers would think was a prayer. It was a whisper of apology to the Imperium.

When he left the Chapel, Veritus was coming down the colonnade. The inquisitor hailed him, and Vangorich waited.

'We're making this into a habit,' he said when Veritus caught up.

'A coincidence is not a habit.'

'Oh.' Not buying it. 'You didn't want to speak to me on a particular subject? No desire to unburden yourself about the Inquisition's internal politics? No?' Veritus looked straight ahead. Vangorich matched his pace. 'What a shame. Then I'll have to content myself with the simple pleasure of your company.'

They reached the corner and turned north.

The grey-brown dawn trickled through skylights to the courtyard.

'A big day,' Vangorich commented. The embarkation was almost complete. The launch of the Merchants' Armada was imminent.

Veritus said, 'A dark one.'

'On that, we can agree.'

They walked past the first of the columns.

Machtannin looked through the sights of the rifle. He had been motionless since Vangorich had entered the chapel ordinary. His finger held the trigger. He did not approve of assassinations. They were distasteful, the province of the Officio Assassinorum. They were too merciful. Targets who did not know they were about to die escaped proper retribution. Machtannin preferred to hide in plain sight, face and dress transformed to appear before the enemies of the Imperium in a guise that inspired confidence. There was a satisfying justice in making traitors feel the sting of betrayal themselves. He had undergone so many polymorphine treatments that his face now was an approximation of his original features. It was a small sacrifice. In exchange, he saw the look on the faces of the guilty as punishment came for them.

He wouldn't see that here. But then Vangorich was no traitor. He was guilty of poor judgement. His mistakes were harming the Imperium, but he believed himself to be virtuous. He would die in that belief. Machtannin supposed he was worthy of that much mercy.

Vangorich and Veritus walked between the first set of columns. The shot was clear.

Veritus paused, as if struck by a sudden thought.

Vangorich walked another two steps, then stopped. 'What is it?' he asked.

Machtannin's concentration narrowed to the centre of Vangorich's forehead. His finger tightened.

The rifle was yanked from his grasp. The stock slammed his head backwards. He rolled into a crouch and jumped to his feet, blinking away the stun. A man stood in the shadows of the wall. He had bent the barrel of the rifle.

'Throne save us from amateurs,' the man said.

Strong, Machtannin thought. Maybe not fast. He leapt at the man, striking with enhanced reflexes. Speed was his weapon. He had once deflected a traitor's bolter shell with the edge of his hand. He landed four blows to the side of the man's neck before the other could even drop the gun.

It was like hitting a column.

The Assassin punched him in the chest. He was fast, too. The hit came before Machtannin could think to evade. Something crunched.

He entered a land of surprise. He was surprised that he wasn't sent flying. He stumbled back from his opening. He tried to attack again, and was surprised when his legs didn't obey his command. He was surprised when they folded up beneath him and he sat down hard. He was surprised to find he was holding his breath.

No.

Surprise: there was no breath to be had.

Surprise: the pain bursting from his chest, the pressure in his skull spreading red and black.

His head rocked forward. There was a hole in his chest. A big one.

Surprise.

Had he seen something in the man's fist?

He couldn't think any more. He couldn't care any more. No more surprises.

And after a great flare, no more pain.

Only the dark.

'Were you waiting for someone?' Vangorich asked as they walked on.

'No.' The hesitation was very brief.

Vangorich smiled. 'Just as well. He won't be coming.'

Later, in his quarters, Vangorich said to Beast Krule, 'Good to have you back.'

Krule grunted. 'This is getting messy,' he said.

'Can't be helped.' Vangorich held a bottle of amasec, debating. An Iaxian vintage, three centuries old. Was there ever the correct occasion for such a treasure? He decided there was, when there might soon be no more occasions at all. He opened the bottle and decanted two glasses. 'Well done,' he said, handing one to Krule.

'Wasn't difficult. They took the bait.'

'Let's not call it bait. I really had hoped Veritus wouldn't push things this far. Think of it as a designated opportunity. If they were going to take action, better it be in a situation we could neutralise.'

Krule shrugged. 'Call it what you like.' He sipped the amasec, and gave an appreciative nod. 'Do you want me to do more?'

'Not yet. I think we have Veritus contained, at least for now. He's running out of allies and moves. Has Wienand reached the Inquisitorial Fortress?'

'I lost track of her before she did. But we'd know if she hadn't.'

'Then we wait to see her move,' Vangorich said. 'That's where we stand.' He turned to the narrow window of his chambers. The strong winds of the day were granting him rare glimpses of the evening sky. The ork moon was there, the executioner's sword half-concealed by the spires of the Imperial Palace. There were also faint glints like moving stars: the larger ships of the Merchants' Armada manoeu-vring. 'And we wait to see what Juskina Tull is about to reap for all of us.'

TWELVE

Klostra – Klostra Primus colony

With a battering crash of iron and cannon and bladed siege shield, the Vindicators rolled through the wreckage of the colony. They came in the wake of the bombardment. The battle tanks were the follow-up to the Iron Warriors' initial charge.

The charge that had already turned into a retreat.

The tanks, Kalkator vowed, would turn the tide. They had before. The *Araakite Doom*, the *Barban Falk*, the *Pyres of Olympia*, and the *Lochos*.

They had fought on Terra, and on Sebastus IV. The blood of Loyalists had sunk into the grain of the metal and the joints of the treads. Statues lined the edges of their hulls. They were the representations of saints and generals, the Imperium's heroes of war and of faith. Now they were defaced, broken. Heads leaned back as if to gaze in horror at the brutality of the universe. Limbs were shattered, replaced with barbed wire. They were the trophies of smashed sieges past, and the promise of fallen cities to come. Behind, the

Demolisher cannons curved massive horns in the image of the Iron Warriors' helms. The guns fired as soon as the tanks approached the remains of the wall. They were siege weapons, designed to reduce defences to lost hopes. Today, they were coming to break a siege.

That fact was an offence to Kalkator's pride and to the proper order of things. He could not make the situation otherwise through will alone. So he would exact retribution for the insult from the bodies of the orks.

The cannon fire hit the ork advance, four shells simultaneously. The explosion was huge. Scores of the enemy vanished and the front half of one of the ork tanks disintegrated. Another kept moving, but on an erratic course, enveloped in flame. It was as if a giant scythe had culled the forward lines of the enemy infantry. The bombardment had done nothing to slow the orks, but now, for a moment, Kalkator saw a hole open up in their formation.

He and his brothers had been forced back to the ruins of Klostra Prime. The bulk of the Great Company had been using the fallen walls of the central manufactorum as a bulwark against the orks. Now they pushed forward again.

The warsmith headed for the *Pyres of Olympia*. As he ran, he sent a stream of bolter fire ahead. Orks fell before him, their heads bursting. A few steps from the *Olympia*, he slammed into a massive brute whose armour had saved it from his shells. He knocked the ork off balance and thrust his chainsword forward, plunging it between skull plate and jaw guard, grinding through the ork's nose and then its skull and brain. He blasted another foe coming at him from the right while he withdrew the blade from the corpse, before leaping to the roof of the *Olympia*. Varravo and Caesax followed him. Other Iron Warriors climbed to the roof of the other tanks while the rest ran close, tearing up the infantry.

We're trying to stop the ocean with a knife, Kalkator thought. Four Vindicators and the individual strength of the brothers of the Great Company was enough to shatter the walls of any fortress, but he had no illusions about their position now. Thousands of orks had already climbed the top of the plateau. Even if the Iron Warriors' counter-attack repelled them, the oncoming force was many times that size. The orks had already landed an infinite infantry.

Their heavy armour on immediate approach was no match for the Vindicators, though. Kalkator wanted to cripple the ork vehicles, and perhaps buy the company time to cohere again. Recreate the wedge, drive into the ork infantry, cause damage to force a retreat.

Impossibility was irrelevant. Impossibility was the bloody constant of the Iron Warriors' history. As ever, there was nothing to do but fight.

At least their wars were their own now, as were the spoils. And even now they weren't cowering behind walls, hoping for the battle to pass, like the bastard sons of Dorn.

The tanks kept firing. After the first great blast, the squadron staggered the volleys, hitting the orks with a continuous string of explosions. The orks slowed, a bit. They did not stop. The tide flowed around the craters, ignoring losses, rushing to the challenge of the Vindicators.

'All fire on the tanks,' Kalkator voxed. 'Base, maintain bombardment one thousand metres forward of initial target zone.'

Three more ork tanks were gutted. The first of the Battle-wagons to reach Klostra Prime had traded thicker armour for speed, and the Vindicators' cannons could take down walls wider than the tanks themselves. The Battlewagons were big, but they crumpled and burned when the Demolisher shells hit them. The ork vehicles had numbers, though. Line after line of them mounted the slope to the colony. They fired back. High explosives flared against the siege shields. Three of the Battlewagons trained their guns on the *Lochos*. Two died trying, but the third flanked the *Lochos* and gutted it.

Over the vox, Derruo snarled in agony. Kalkator glanced back. Two other battle-brothers had been blown apart, but Derruo, his armour scorched black, his left leg dragging, was still in the fight.

The *Olympia* was out in front now. Behind it, the *Araakite Doom* avenged the *Lochos* with a shot that hit the ork tank's fuel reserves at almost point-blank range. The warmth of the fire washed over the squadron.

Kalkator cursed as a shell clipped the top of the siege shield. He leaned forward into the wash of the explosion. It took out the ork that had just vaulted up from the front of the tank. More of the brutes followed. Kalkator, Varravo and Caesax moved forward on the roof. They turned their chainswords on the orks who made it past the *Pyres of Olympia*'s sponson bolters. The tank's horns were magma cutters, taking down still more of the foe. The ground was littered with bisected corpses.

And the orks kept coming.

'What do they want with the place?' Varravo voxed. 'There's nothing left.'

'They want us,' said Kalkator. Whatever other designs the orks might have for Klostra, their targets now were the Iron Warriors. Perhaps the planet had some other value. If it did, that was secondary to the promise of war. Kalkator had used the mortal colonists as loyal bait. He wondered now if the orks hadn't done the same to him, luring the company in with the illusion that there was a possible strategy here.

To the north, the great artillery explosions continued. A curtain of smoke, flame and raining debris rose between the Iron Warriors and the approaching body of the ork host. The Great Company and its Vindicators advanced further into the flesh and over the machinery of the enemy. They were almost at the base of the wall now.

'Warsmith,' voxed Occillax, piloting the *Olympia*, 'do we descend the slope?'

Kalkator never answered. His command was interrupted by a rolling wave of sound, the thunder of a mountain cracking in half. He looked back. In the distance, in the direction of the base, a volcanic glow lit the deep twilight that passed for day on Klostra. The rumble had a rhythm. Streaks of light cut through black clouds towards the glow. An orbital bombardment.

'Klostra Base, report,' Kalkator voxed. He called three more times, as he looked away and kept killing orks. Silence from the base.

And silence from the guns.

The artillery barrage ended. Occillax halted the *Pyres of Olympia*. The curtain faded. The wrecking yard of ork vehicles appeared and so did the forces that were coming on, the ones untouched by the Iron Warriors cannons.

Four super-heavies. Tanks twice the size of the Vindicators, their guns with bores as wide as Demolishers, but the length of autocannons. As if they had been waiting for their proper introduction, they opened fire now.

They had the rate of autocannons, too.

And as the *boom* of greenskin ordnance battered the plateau of Klostra Primus, greater silhouettes yet loomed behind the battle fortresses. Colossi, three of them, greenskin idols fifty metres tall. They rocked side to side as they marched over machine and kin, a manufactorum's worth of smoke belching from the chimneys rising from their backs. Flame gouted from their jaws. Their eyes were energy weapon turrets, blazing red lightning. The right arm of each terminated in a hand whose fingers were linked cannons, four strong. The left arm of one was a hammer the size of a tank. The second had a chainblade fifteen metres long. The third wielded a claw that could tear the hills apart.

Beneath the roars of the engines, the beat of the cannons and the tectonic rumble of the orbital strikes, Kalkator heard another sound. It would have been inaudible if it hadn't come from a hundred thousand ork throats in unison.

'They're laughing at us,' said Caesax.

Why wouldn't they? Kalkator thought through his rage. The orks were bringing down a compounded humiliation on the Great Company. They attacked with overwhelming numbers, unstoppable armament, and then outmanoeuvred the Iron Warriors. In the gap between realising the doom of Klostra and bringing his blade down on still another ork skull, he understood that the orks were sending a message. They were speaking through the language of annihilation, and what they said was, *Behold what we can do. We are more powerful and more clever than you. You are nothing.*

If hate alone were a force, he would have incinerated the planet in that moment.

'Pull back,' he ordered.

'Where to?' Caesax asked.

'The mountains.'

'Towards an orbital bombardment?'

'It will be finished by the time we get there,' he snarled.

They retreated towards oblivion.

Deep into the remains of the settlement, tens of thousands of blackened mortal corpses on all sides, the vox came alive with the first extra-planetary contact since the ork moon tore through space into Klostra's orbit. It came from the strike cruisers *Palimodes* and *Scythe of Schravaan*. The gravity storms had destroyed all of the company's fleet at anchor. The two cruisers had been at the Ostrom outpost, and had been silent since the initial vox-failure on Klostra. They had not been recalled. Kalkator didn't know why they had returned. He didn't care.

He interrupted the torrent of shouted questions from the bridges. 'I want the full complement of Thunderhawks planetside for immediate evacuation of all forces.' He gave coordinates for a position just south of the settlement.

'That moon–' Attonax, on the *Palimodes*, began.

'Do not engage!' Kalkator shouted. The words were toxic. They were echoes of the foulest days of the Iron Warriors' past.

'Enemy launches detected,' Attonax said.

Kalkator roared at the enemy, and the orks roared back. The laughter grew louder. It seemed to him that there was mockery in every attack. Every ork that he cut down died with the belief that it, and not he, was victorious. The giant ork machines heaved into sight over the ruined wall. They were on the plateau. The company moved faster than the ork super-heavies, but the infantry was on all sides, slowing them down. The ork Battlewagons kept pace, pounding the retreating Iron Warriors. The *Pyres of Olympia*, the *Barban Falk* and the *Araakite Doom* moved backwards, keeping their Demolishers trained on the foe. Bolter, cannon and magma cutter tore swaths through infantry and smashed more tanks open. But the waves of the green tide closed over the gaps. And the fire from the ork guns grew more intense.

Brothers died. Kalkator felt no regret when he saw them fall, but he did feel frustration. The orks were eroding his combat strength bit by bit.

There were no gaps in the enemy barrage now. Kalkator could see little but flame and eruptions on all sides. The *Araakite Doom* exploded, and then there were two tanks. '*Palimodes, Scythe of Schravaan*, where is our extraction?' the warsmith demanded.

'Right above you,' came the reply.

Kalkator couldn't see the Thunderhawks in the midst of the ork fire, but his Lyman's ear was able now to distinguish their engines from the din of the enemy machines. A few seconds later, Hellstrike missiles screamed onto the ork tanks, followed by the hard rain of multiple heavy bolters.

For several seconds, the world vanished completely. There was fire, and there was nothing else, and Kalkator grinned, because the flames were on the orks now, and they were learning the price of their arrogance.

He allowed himself that burst of savage pleasure. It lasted as long as the initial flash of the explosions. Then he faced again the reality of defeat, of humiliation, and of the fact that this was not a tide that could be turned by even a hundred Thunderhawks.

The rate of the ork fire dropped. Four more Battlewagons were burning shells.

The Vindicators were moving more and more slowly, providing cover for the battle-brothers on foot. They no longer had their flank escorts. A group of massive orks evaded the sponson fire of the *Olympia* and scrambled up onto the roof to Kalkator's left. Before he could turn, one of them grabbed his left arm with a power claw. It squeezed, cracking the ceramite, crushing servo-motors. It would have broken his arm, had it still been flesh.

It hadn't been for three hundred years. The change had come upon it, the gods of Chaos visiting him with the gift of a string of grasping mouths from shoulder to wrist. He had taken his chainblade to the arm himself, amputating it in his quarters, taking the time to burn the offending limb while his blood poured onto the ship's decking before he stormed off, still steady on his feet, to find the Apothecary. The left arm was bionic now, a thing of metal and barbed ridges. When he didn't buckle, the ork looked surprised.

Kalkator swung his bolter around and shot the ork in the face. The top half of its skull disintegrated, showering the roof of the *Olympia* with blood and brain matter. The claw released Kalkator as the body slumped. He kicked the corpse off the tank and flexed his arm. It moved in jerks, but was still functional.

To the rear, the gunships were landing. Three of the twelve remained in the air, buying time with rockets and shells. The Vindicators slowed to a crawl. Kalkator looked back and saw the first members of the company embarking. He faced forward again and watched time stolen from them.

The huge walkers and the battle fortresses were close. The walkers redirected their fire at the Thunderhawks. To the autocannon bursts were added missile launches from their shoulders. The attacks vectored onto a single target. The gunship's pilot tried to evade. Two missiles hit the starboard wing, shells slammed into the nose, and the gunship dropped.

As it fell, a torrent of flame shot from the jaws of the nearest walker and enveloped the cockpit. The Thunderhawk hit the ground with meteoric force. It collided with one of the battle fortresses, the impact fusing the two behemoths together. Embraced by flame, they became a mountain of clashing metal, a single being that was the madness and destruction of war. They lost shape. The blasts came, shaking the ground so hard that Kalkator was almost knocked off his feet.

Above, a second gunship was trailing smoke, though it still fought. The *Olympia* fired its cannon through the flames of the collision. It hit one of the walkers in the centre of its wide skirt, and the ork titan seemed to stumble, then rocked forwards and came on. Its arms reached towards the Vindicator. Kalkator looked up at the cluster of auto-cannons aimed at his head.

'Off!' he yelled.

He jumped to the right. So did Caesax. Varravo was a beat behind. The cannonade caught him. The *Pyres of Olympia* fired back – still operational, but its roof was slag. Some of the debris was just recognisable as Varravo's ruined armour.

The *Olympia*'s engine whined, but the tank didn't move. 'We've lost guidance,' Occillax voxed.

'Continue the attack,' Kalkator ordered. He cut his way through more ork infantry. The brutes were stunned by the walker's bombardment. Kalkator and Caesax made quick progress towards the rear.

'To what end?'

'Hold them off as best you can, brother.'

'This is pointless.'

'Step outside and I'll kill you myself. Follow your orders.'

Occillax cursed him, but obeyed. Kalkator and Caesax left the Vindicator behind. The slow beat of its cannon resumed. It hit the walker again, and this time the ork Titan responded with its hammer. It struck the *Olympia* hard enough to make the ground shake again. The ork machinery roared louder, in triumph and anger. Another blast from the cannon, another hit to the walker, but the orks crewing the monster were focused on victory, not on the casualties they suffered. The hammer came down again and again, and the third time was when Kalkator heard the shriek of compacting metal. The gun fell silent.

He was the last to reach the landing zone, a few steps behind Caesax. They ran up the ramp to the final gunship, the *Meratara*. Not all of the Thunderhawks had taken off again – the battle fortresses had demolished three of them on the ground. Kalkator didn't know how many troops he had lost in each one. The reckoning would wait until later, if there was a later.

The ramp raised as he reached the top and the Thunderhawk took off. He made his way forward to the cockpit to witness the end. He saw the *Barban Falk* join the *Olympia* in destruction, and another gunship blasted out of the sky. Then they were in the clouds, and though the ship rattled through the turbulence of the atmosphere, there were a few minutes of calm.

They weren't welcome. They gave him time to think, to feel the humiliation of the loss scrape at his pride.

The *Meratara* shot up from the clouds. A new vision appeared before Kalkator. Another humiliation, another great power smashing a weaker one. The *Scythe of Schravaan* was under heavy attack. Squadrons of ork fighters swarmed around it. From the star fortress came an unending stream of rockets. The strike cruiser's void shields flashed and flashed, surrounding the vessel in an aurora of desperation. Its armaments lit the void with anger. Ork vessels died, and rockets exploded short of their target.

Drops in the ocean. There were so many more orks on the way that the space between the moon and the ship seemed full. The *Schravaan*'s death was minutes away.

'Make for the *Palimodes*,' Kalkator told Lerontus, the gunship's pilot. The other strike cruiser, more distant from the star fortress, was holding its own. The orks were amusing themselves with taking down one large prey at a time.

Not all of them were satisfied with the *Schravaan*. Three fighters came at the *Meratara*. Their salvoes hit hard. Warning runes lit up as the hull was pierced in multiple places. Kalkator heard the shriek of atmosphere venting. He drowned it out with his own roar of rage. As Lerontus pulled the gunship up sharply, Kalkator grabbed the controls for the weapons systems.

The fighters looped back for a second pass.

'Straight at them,' Kalkator told Lerontus.

'With pleasure.' The pilot's anger was the mirror of his own.

Kalkator held his fire. Lerontus turned the Thunderhawk into a head-on course towards the ork ships. The orks misjudged the relative speed of the approach and the smaller profile the gunship now presented. A few shots still hit. Kalkator ignored them. He would hold the vessel together with his will if he had to.

The orks bunched closer together, jockeying for the better angle on their prey.

Kalkator fired all forward armament. Thunderhawk cannon, heavy bolters and lascannons struck the centre fighter. It vaporised. The blast washed over the other two ships. Their pilots overcorrected and collided.

The *Meratara* slammed through the cloud of debris, and raced on towards the *Palimodes*.

The other gunships still in flight were following the same path. The mathematics of defeat cascaded through Kalkator's mind. How many had headed to the *Schravaan* first? How many had been taken out before reaching either vessel? How many beyond capacity would Attonax try to take on board? Did he even have to make that decision?

We have been besieged, Kalkator thought. And our citadels have fallen. The bitterness of the reality filled him with frustrated violence. Had there been a serf within reach, he would have torn the mortal apart just to see the blood.

The Thunderhawk was on the final approach to the *Palimodes* when the end came to the *Scythe of Schravaan*. Kalkator didn't see what caused the fatal blow. It happened on the ship's starboard, which faced towards the moon. Searing white lit the void. It engulfed the *Schravaan*'s midsection, a fist of suns. The bow and stern began to move independently, and the light faded, resolving into a halo of individual explosions. A gap formed between the fore and aft halves of the ship before the bow began a spiral away from the stern. The movement was slow, graceful. The lights of the void shields went dark. In their place, lines of flames, the angry red of infected veins, raced down the bow's length as it fell towards Klostra's atmosphere.

The reactor blew, a second wound of light in the void. The reach of the blast was enormous, wiping the near space clean of ork fighters. That death-cry bought the *Palimodes* a bit more time. Kalkator dared to think a portion of the Great Company might extract itself from the system. The loss wouldn't be total.

Then he watched the *Schravaan*'s bow become a torch as it hit Klostra's atmosphere, and he thought he could hear the laughter of the orks even here.

The *Palimodes*' engines were going hot as the Thunderhawk docked. Attonax had ordered the run. The ship was racing to the system's Mandeville point when Kalkator walked onto the bridge. He joined Attonax at the command throne. The other Iron Warrior nodded to him and vacated the throne.

'The ship is yours, warsmith,' he said.

For as long as we have one, Kalkator thought. The first rocket hits were beginning. The rear shields were holding strong, though, and the *Palimodes* was picking up speed. 'Set course for the Ostrom System,' he said.

'We can't,' Attonax told him. 'We've lost it too.'

'What?'

'That's why we returned.' His face was a patchwork of metal and flesh, iron replacing the mutations excavated from his skull. Expression was difficult. His bitterness was profound, for it to be so apparent. 'We were retreating.'

'The orks hit us there too?'

'No. The Black Templars.'

The Great Company was caught between two fronts. Kalkator's forces had lost their holdings. He grimaced.

'Get us to the point and make the jump,' he ordered.

'Where to?' Attonax asked.

Kalkator didn't answer. He watched the strategium screens, noting the damage reports as they came in, measuring them against what he knew the ship could take; tallying still more casualties, still more strength leeched from his command.

The deck vibrated: rocket hits overwhelming the void shields. The sensorium array registered ork torpedo ships in pursuit. The *Palimodes* accelerated. The Mandeville point drew closer.

'Our integrity...' Attonax began.

'Will be enough,' Kalkator finished. 'If we're breathing, we jump.'

The other Iron Warrior nodded. If the ship died, it would not be in the sight of the orks.

The moment of the transition came. The writhe of the warp appeared on the primary oculus. The *Palimodes* was racing through nothing to nowhere.

'The Navigator will need a destination,' Attonax said.

'I'm aware of that.' He stared at the violence of colliding absences and clawed potential. 'We can't fight them both,' he said.

There was a long silence. At last, Attonax asked, 'What are you saying?'

'That we can't fight them both.'

THIRTEEN

Terra – the Imperial Palace

Juskina Tull had a view of the Fields of Winged Victory from her quarters. The armourglass window stretched across the entire width of the reception chamber. The room was the largest of her suite, occupying half of the top floor of the Pharos Tower. The size was not an indulgence. Nor was its collection of tapestries that draped the opposite wall. This display, drawn from holdings of works from across the Imperium, changed daily. A necessary ritual. The furniture underwent a similar change. There was always a large dining table, and seats for dozens. It was the individual identities of the items that altered.

Sometimes Tull took an active part in the selections of the day. Sometimes she left it to the serfs. What was important was the display. Any guest would see the riches of Imperial trade, and the vast reach of the Chartist fleet. Repeat guests witnessed ever greater wealth through perpetual variety. The more important the visitors, the more often they came, and the more they would be dizzied by the unending parade.

The symbolic, Tull understood, was not weaker than the real. The symbolic shaped the real. In the right hands, it was a weapon. Some of the other High Lords grasped the principle. Mesring certainly did. But his view was blinkered. He couldn't see beyond the icons. He could only understand symbols that derived their potency through connection to the God-Emperor.

Then there was Lansung. A hopeless case. He could see the symbolic value in military action. He couldn't imagine the reverse.

'Gazing upon your good work?' the Lord High Admiral asked.

Tull turned away from the window. She nodded at Georg Steinert, her majordomo. He withdrew.

'I was,' she said to Lansung.

'Proud of yourself, aren't you.'

'Proud of us all. This is a great moment.'

He snorted. 'Well, you can enjoy it without me.'

'What do you mean?'

'I won't have any part of the deployment.'

'The *Autocephalax Eternal...*'

'It will remain on station.'

'You realise what that will look like.' She was pleased that she answered without pause, as if his decision made no difference. Perhaps it didn't.

'Yes.' The exhaustion in that single syllable was immense. At some point, Lansung appeared to have crossed the line between humiliation and apathy.

'You're a coward,' Tull said, making sure Lansung understood what was heading his way.

'I'm not here to posture,' he said.

'I know you're not. I'm telling you simple truths. If you back out of the Proletarian Crusade, I'll destroy you.'

'Threats now.'

'Just the truth. Like I said.'

Lansung shrugged. 'Threats,' he repeated. 'Empty ones.'

'Is that a dare?' she asked.

He shook his head. 'Just the truth, since that's what we're speaking. You won't destroy me. The orks will take care of that when they arrive. I'll outlive your fleet of fools, though. I notice that you're not accompanying them.'

'I'm not a military commander.'

'No. You most certainly are not.'

She smiled. 'I sense there is a point you're making, Admiral.'

He gave her a hard, tired stare. 'I've already made it.' He turned to go.

'You know I will destroy you,' she said.

He stopped. 'I know you can. But why? Out of spite?'

'You know me better than that.'

'I thought I did.'

'You are sabotaging something too important.'

'Bold words.'

'The truth.'

He walked to the door. 'As you say. But important to Terra or to you?'

'Get out.'

She went back to the window. She heard Steinert show

Lansung out. She looked towards the Fields of Winged Victory and took a breath. Lansung would have been pleased to see that it was unsteady.

He would be wrong to think he had rattled her. She had been bracing to face hard questions when he arrived. No, she wasn't a military commander. She was aware of that. Yet this was a campaign that she had mounted, and that she was directing. She had Verreault and Zeck on board, but she had to be cautious about using them as resources. She had arranged to have the Astra Militarum regiments spread out through the Armada as a means to provide some structure to the civilian troops. But the move also diluted Verreault's leverage. He, Zeck, Mesring, Ekharth – all of the allies in the Crusade had some pull, but only she had control of the Armada itself. The captains answered to her, so she had final say on disposition and launch.

And tactics.

The plan of attack was not a sophisticated one. Then again, if it was, it couldn't be carried out. The ships were crewed by merchants. There were able pilots aboard many, pilots who had brought their ships through threats as lethal as any faced by the Imperial Navy. Their skills, though, were individual. They had no experience fighting in formation. They fled conflict. They didn't seek it out.

She asked herself the question she had been avoiding since first announcing the Proletarian Crusade. Was she making a mistake? She made herself think through the consequences. She ran through possible balance sheets, measuring investment against risk, potential gain against possible loss.

She was oddly reassured.

If the Crusade failed, political damage would be the least of her problems. Retribution would be far from anyone else's mind. Defeat would mean the loss of everything. Success, however, would place her in an unchallengeable position. That was the equation, then: victory of the Armada meant her personal victory, while defeat meant no one else would be the victor. There was no question. This was the smart move.

It was also so much more than that. She believed in what she was doing.

The crowd in the Fields was the biggest yet seen. The people there now were not volunteers. The last of those had embarked hours ago. Gathered now were celebrants, well-wishers, families. The excited, the curious, the hopeful. The desperate. They were all the desperate.

Tull had given them hope. She had given all of Terra hope. That was a singular achievement. She was proud of it. This was Terra's greatest crisis since the Siege, the worst moment in the living memory of every human being on the planet. The plague of despair had been upon them, Zeck's Adeptus Arbites had been unable to end the panic, and she, with a single speech, had turned the tide. She had given the billions determination, direction, purpose. An endeavour of legend had sprung into being at her urging, and despite the doubts of Vangorich and Lansung, it was not a folly. Lack of action would have been a folly. And what other options were there? The cry for help had gone out, but there were no elements of the Navy or the Adeptus Astartes that could reach Terra in time.

How do you know? That was the question she could not answer. It kept prying open her doubts. She closed them again with reason. Whatever cause the orks had for waiting, they would not wait until help had arrived. Tull thought it likely that the orks believed they had already won, and had the leisure of invading when it best suited them.

She walked across the chamber to the door. It was time to head to the Great Chamber. Time for another speech. Time to show the orks that they were wrong.

Time to launch.

'We're going in on that?' Kord asked.

Their shuttle was drawing up to the *Militant Fire*'s landing bay.

'What did you expect?' said Haas. 'A grand cruiser?'

'Of course not. But this... It's so small.'

He was right.

'I can see even smaller,' she pointed out.

'That makes me feel a lot better.' He craned his head to look up through the viewing block next to his bench. He squirmed in the grav-harness. 'I was hoping for maybe one of the mass conveyors.' He pointed to something Haas couldn't see from her angle. 'They'll be carrying thousands.'

'No room for everyone on them. They're mainly reserved for Imperial Guard companies, from what I heard.'

'I know that,' he said, irritable. 'I was just saying what I'd hoped. Those ships are strong. They can take some hits. This will get swatted in the first seconds of the attack. We're cannon fodder.'

'That's a revelation to you?'

He shrugged. He didn't look at her, watching as the shuttle entered the *Fire*'s bay.

Haas said, 'What did you think was going to happen when we joined this endeavour?'

Another shrug.

'Look at me,' she said.

He did. His jaw was set. There was doubt in his eyes.

'I didn't want to join the Crusade,' she said. 'I thought our duty was to the maintenance of the law, and nothing else.'

'I'm sorry–' he began.

She held up a hand. 'Let me finish. You were right. I was wrong. This is what we're supposed to be doing. If we win, we preserve Terra and the law. If we lose, both are gone. I'm proud to be here, Ottmar. You should be too. I don't have any illusions about what's going to happen, though. Nor should you. Yes, we're cannon fodder. Of course we are. So is every single member of the Crusade. No exceptions.' The shuttle came to a halt with the bang of landing struts on the deck. The engines cut out. Haas undid her harness and leaned forward. 'That's why this might work,' she said. 'No one element of the Armada is more important than another. It doesn't matter who gets through, as long as enough of us do.' She stood up. 'There's a reason cannon fodder is used. It works.'

Kord remained seated. The shuttle's side door opened. Hydraulics hissed as its boarding ramp lowered to the deck. The squad of Jupiter Storm disembarked first. The other thirty passengers followed. Other than Haas and Kord, they were all civilians. Haas wanted to be out in front of them, but Kord was unmoving. 'Ottmar?' she said.

'So glorious deaths await us,' Kord said. He was hoarse. His voice was thin.

She clapped him on the shoulder. 'Important ones, anyway. Let's go.'

His face looked as it did when the ork moon had become visible over the Fields of Winged Victory. Haas had never had cause to question Kord's courage or his dedication to duty. She was dismayed that he was forcing her to do so now. 'What's wrong?' she asked. Death had been no stranger in their years of enforcing the Emperor's law.

His lips moved. His whisper was too faint.

'What?' Haas said. She leaned forward.

'It's too big,' Kord repeated. 'We're too small.'

She understood him, then. She wished she hadn't. He drew his confidence from his faith in the strength of the greater body that he represented. He was a terror on the streets because he felt the might of the Adeptus Arbites behind him. But now, when he acted for the survival of the Imperium itself, he did not believe it was strong enough to defeat the orks.

'Stand up,' she told him.

He obeyed, shame and pleading contorting his features.

She stalked out of the shuttle and down the ramp. She was disgusted, but he still wore the uniform of an Arbitrator. She would not allow him to disgrace it in her presence.

Kord followed her.

There were about five hundred souls in the cargo bay. Most of them were civilian. There was a scattering of Arbitrators from other precincts. Haas counted three squads of the Jupiter Storm. They were looking at the people who would be their charges with bemused scepticism.

The captain of the *Militant Fire* appeared on a platform overlooking the bay, flanked by his first mate. He started to speak, but was drowned out by the babble of conversation on the floor. The woman, her bearing marking her as a Guard veteran, put two fingers in her mouth and whistled for silence.

'Thank you, First Officer Kondos,' the captain said. To his human cargo, he said, 'Welcome. My name is Leander Narkissos, and I'll have the honour of transporting you into battle.'

His manner was easy. He struck Haas as a man who had consciously shed his illusions, and was at peace with the reality of his situation. That was a good sign, she thought. He would be less likely to panic under fire. Despite what she had said to Kord, she still liked the idea of some possibility of survival.

Narkissos continued, 'I'm going to wager that a few – just a few – of you were a bit disheartened when you beheld the warlike majesty of the *Militant Fire*.' He waited for the laughter to subside. 'I don't blame you. I would probably feel the same.' He straightened, becoming more formal, his posture almost martial. 'Let me say this. We aren't a big ship. Our armour is weak. But we're fast. We're nimble. If you examined the history of the *Fire* by the cold light of rationality, you would have to conclude that she should have been destroyed many times over. Are the odds against us? Absolutely. There is no reason to believe we'll live one more day.' A sly grin crept over his face. 'Which is precisely why I say that our odds are excellent.'

No laughter this time. Only cheers. Haas joined in.

She had never expected to take such delight in madness. Beside her, Kord had fallen into the silent misery of sanity.

Juskina Tull, the Speaker for the Chartist Captains, rose in the Great Chamber and began to speak. Pict feeds flashed her image and her words across the planet. The speech was one she had laboured over since the beginning of the Crusade. She had rehearsed it for days. She knew that its delivery was the most important performance of her life. At an abstract level, she also knew that it might be one of the last. She knew this, but did not believe it. The destruction of Terra and her own death were impossible. She feared the loss of prestige, and being beholden to her enemies. But not extermination.

'Fellow Lords, members of the Senatorum, citizens of Terra. We stand together in a moment of great peril and greater pride. A very short time ago, I asked for your help. You answered. You answered in such numbers and with such fervour that, did they but deserve it, I would pity the orks.'

That was how she began. She spoke for fifteen minutes. She spoke of the bravery of the individual, of the power of the many. She spoke of humility and pride. By the end, she thundered, promising that legendary doom was coming to the orks.

It was a fine speech. It addressed the fears of the populace, and sought to calm them. It articulated their hopes, and sought to stoke them. It was the greatest work of a politician who knew that oratory was an art form, and whose mastery of the medium was unchallenged.

Juskina Tull's speech was written to shape the departure

of the Armada into an event whose celebration would shake the heavens with its fervour. Was it not, when all was said and done, Terra's last chance for hope?

When Tull spoke, her intent was to ignite rapture.

Seated on the central dais of the Great Chamber, Vangorich admired Tull's artistry. Even he was stirred by the words, though their very potency filled him with dread. They were words of enormous meaning. Hearing them meant that the Proletarian Crusade had begun. Its consequences would be coming soon.

Lord High Admiral Lansung heard the speech from the bridge of the *Autocephalax Eternal*. He had come to his flagship directly from Tull's quarters. He had no intention of being in her sight at her moment of triumph, and giving her even more reason to gloat. He was here too because of his own dread. He counted Vangorich as an enemy, but the old assassin was right – the Crusade would end in disaster. However, as he listened to the speech he found himself hoping that he was wrong. He had no wish to face the reality of attempting the defence of Terra with just the flagship and its escort. He knew how that would end.

With every word Tull spoke, Lansung's throat dried. The conviction grew that he would see his great fear realised.

In the Fields of Winged Victory, hundreds of thousands watched the pict feed of Tull. They listened with the hunger of the starving. When she finished her speech, and the underbelly of the low, toxic clouds over the Imperial Palace lit up with a fireworks display worthy of the victory at Ullanor, the people roared. The roar was as loud as on the day Tull had announced the crusade, but it was not the same kind of cheer at all. That moment had been the rebirth of hope when all had seemed lost. This moment was when the dream of the Crusade became real. The Merchants' Armada carried all hope with it. It was the last chance. It was the last wall. In the soul of every human on Terra, regardless of belief, was the hard knowledge of how fragile the last wall was.

The roar was painful. It made throats ragged. It was the refusal to fall into a final night, and it was the fear that the end was inevitable. It was the holding on to a belief with a fatal, slippery grasp.

It was, in a word, desperation.

The people cheered, and they kept cheering. Many of them were weeping. Some wished they were on the ships, heading for battle, but there was no more room. Others were relieved to be where they were, and cheered because doing so held off, for a little bit longer, the awful experience of waiting that would follow next.

The masses in the Fields of Winged Victory tried to draw strength from their numbers, and from the volume of their shout. But the sky had cleared again towards the end of Tull's speech, and they could see the stars, and the lights of the fleet, and they could see the ork moon, and they felt the awful hollowness of hope. So they shouted even louder, shouted until they were hoarse, shouted until they fell to their knees, gagging over the pain of a simple breath. They did not find strength in each other. They saw and heard and felt only their own fear reflected back at them a hundred thousand times. They shouted as if that might help them stay afloat in the wave of desperation.

But they sank. And they drowned.

In the shadow of the Tower of the Hegemon; in the corridors of the administrative complex, larger than a nation state, of the Estates Imperium; in the tangled warrens of the Opifex hive districts, where the uncountable legions of architects, stonemasons and other Palace artisans dwelt; half a world away, at the base of the Eternity Gate; across the millions of square kilometres of the Imperial Palace, the people stopped in their tasks and their prayers and their tears and listened. On the other side of the globe, in the vastness of the Ecclesiarchal Palace, they listened. Even in the Inquisitorial Fortress, Tull was heard and seen. In every corner of Holy Terra, singly or in groups, the people sought comfort in the words and in Tull's magisterial, triumphal bearing. Singly or in groups, they came face to face with their desperation.

The planet resounded with a cry as fierce, as expressive of the collective pain as the scream that had greeted the arrival of the star fortress. This was not terror, but it was the fear of terror's return. It was the dying patient's clutch at the chimera of a cure. It was the shout that would serve as battle cry for all the billions who would not be in the war until the war came for them.

It was desperation.

It was sinking.

It was drowning.

On the thousands of ships that made up the Merchants' Armada, the crews and volunteers and Astra Militarum heard the speech too. They did not pay it quite as much heed. They had other matters to draw their attention.

The ships were moving. They were powering up engines. They were leaving anchor. They moved in a rough formation. They were heading into battle. For the volunteers, the reality of their choice had come. Many of them experienced the vertiginous sensation of running off a precipice, and feeling the sudden absence of firm ground beneath their feet. Some of them were sick.

In the *Militant Fire*'s observation dome, Galatea Haas looked out into the void as vessels beyond counting began to travel in concert. The ork moon was straight ahead. It was not drawing closer yet. Even so, it seemed larger. She looked at its surface, and pictured fighting there. She tried to will the *Fire* past the ork defences to the commencement of the invasion. Until moonfall, there was no action she could take that would at least give her the illusion of mastery over her fate. For now, she had to wait, and place her life in the hands of Narkissos and his crew.

There was no sign of Kord. He had barely set foot out of the cargo bay since their arrival. Haas exchanged a look with the soldiers a few paces to her right. They wore the mustard uniform and red sash of the Jupiter Storm. Beneath her armour, so did she. All the Crusaders aboard the *Militant Fire* had been inducted into that regiment. Braylon Gattan was a captain in the 546th Jupiter Storm, and the lone officer of that rank on the *Fire*. Beside him was his commissar, Deklan Sever, quite a bit older. They nodded to her. They were feeling the same hard impatience. At least she was here, she thought, on this ship. At least she was part of a massive move against the orks. She was glad. She had no regrets.

Behind her, the speech continued. Tull built to a crescendo of fervour. The ship moved faster, as if it too were responding to her words. The Armada, brought into being by the determination of the Speaker for the Chartist Captains, gathered momentum. Its formation became more and more defined. It was no longer a confusing cluster of disparate vessels. It took on the shape of a wide spearhead. The ships became the components of the great weapon.

'The strength of Terra approaches the enemy, carrying dread before it,' said Tull.

It left dread behind it, too.

On Terra, the people knew that many, perhaps most (but by the Throne, please, not all) of the heroes of the Proletarian Crusade would die. But if those deaths were exchanged for an end to the hellish moon, then they would be celebrated. It was not the deaths that were dreaded. It was their futility.

The fleet did not carry dread within it. There was too much determination.

But it did carry desperation.

Desperation given the shape of metal, given power, given impetus, given speed – but little armour and few weapons – the Armada moved away from its orbital position. The greatest civilian mobilisation in Terra's history swept towards the orks.

FOURTEEN

Terra – the Inquisitorial Fortress

Wienand and Rendenstein approached the main gates, striding along the centre of the Sigillite's March. The time for secrecy was past. Even if their arrival was not expected, trying to gain access to the Inquisitorial Fortress by any means other than the direct one would be suicidal. What was more, Wienand was clear on the message she wanted to send. She had nothing to hide. She was not a fugitive. She, and no one else, was the Inquisitorial Representative to the Senatorum, and it was in that capacity that she was here, beneath the polar ice cap, in the vast caverns that housed the concentrated might of the Inquisition.

The March ran in a straight line through a cave big enough to swallow a battleship. They were too far underground for the endless cold of the surface to reach them. Even so, the air in the cavern was icy. Wienand's breath misted. The sound of her boot heels was hollow with chill.

The Sigillite's March was a hundred metres wide, and a thousand long. The wiring embedded in the flagstones formed a massive interlocking system of hexagrammic wards. The density of the sigils was such that the path as a whole functioned as a gigantic null generator. Iron pillars rose every ten metres, their powerful lumen globes turning the March into a shining road through darkness. There were no barriers on either side, only the shadows of the cavern. The brilliant light of the March was another primary defence. It made conventional weapons pointless. The individuals who walked the March were blind to anything beyond its edges, but eyes in the dark watched them. To travel the kilometre of the March was to be vulnerable at every level: psychic abilities shut down, in the open, unable to see potential attacks.

For Wienand, the fifteen-minute stroll was a declaration of faith in her position. She was announcing to the many who watched that she was confident about reaching the doors unharmed. Rendenstein walked one step behind her, arms at her side, hands open. She didn't have to be carrying a weapon to be considered a threat. She had to keep her movements as innocuous as possible.

'This is difficult for you, I know,' Wienand said when they were halfway along.

'I don't like being neutralised. There's no way for me to protect you here.'

'This is the one place I don't need protection.'

Rendenstein grunted, sceptical.

'That wasn't a lie,' Wienand reassured her. 'If something was going to happen, it would have already.'

'That makes me feel so much better.'

'It should. It means we have arrived safely, and that

there is a solid chance that the purpose of the journey will succeed.'

Rendenstein didn't reply. Wienand glanced over her shoulder. Her bodyguard looked thoughtful.

The main doors to the Fortress loomed ahead. They were built into a wall that extended into the cavern's night in both directions. The doors expressed both the Inquisition's power and its secretive nature. They were massive, wrought iron in appearance, though those were plates fixed to adamantium. The rosette of the Inquisition occupied the centre of the two doors, bisected by the seam between them, and extended to their full ten-metre height.

There was no practical reason for the doors to be so monumental, so authoritative. No one would ever see them except the inquisitors, or those rare prisoners, as unfortunate as they were privileged, whose sight of the door was their assurance of execution once their usefulness was at an end. The Inquisitorial Fortress was a keep that not only had never been stormed, it had never been besieged. But it was prepared. And it would announce to any foe the folly of attack, and the respect that was due to the servants of the Imperium within.

A lone figure waited for Wienand, standing before the base of the rosette. He was in full dress plate. His ceramite carapace armour was draped by a cloak of crimson and black. A sash of the same colours crossed his chest from left shoulder to the sheath of his sword. Gold wards marked his pauldrons and chestplate, and there were more on his plasma pistol's holster.

'Greetings, Castellan Kober,' Wienand said.

'Inquisitor Wienand,' he answered. His stance, his expression, his tone and his words were neutral.

She had expected Henrik Kober to be her main obstacle. He wouldn't deny her entry, but he might have the clout to block anything she tried to accomplish. The position of Castellan was a rotating one, changing every year or upon the death of the serving inquisitor. The office had no formal political power over other inquisitors. Its mandate was the defence of the Fortress. The administrative authority that followed from that was considerable, and so, then, was the indirect influence wielded by the Castellan. The yearly rotation ensured that none of the holders of the appointment had the time to establish personal dominance to any degree that couldn't be undone by the next Castellan. But for that year, there was clout.

Wienand decided to force the issue immediately. There wasn't time for subtlety. She had heard Tull's speech during the final leg of her journey. 'Are we going to be in conflict?' she asked.

'There have been serious questions raised about you.'

'But no charges,' she said, noting that he hadn't answered her question.

'Not yet,' he admitted. Then he said, 'Inquisitor van der Deckart is dead. Inquisitor Machtannin has been assassinated. And there has been an attempt on Inquisitor Veritus' life.'

'And on mine,' she pointed out. She was startled to hear about Machtannin. She guessed Vangorich had been at work. 'I make no accusations,' she continued. 'I have no interest in a pointless battle. And if you think I organised assassination missions while making my way here, then I must be very formidable.'

'I don't think what happened was at your command,' Kober said. 'I do think the deaths had something to do with you.'

'If they did, and I am responsible, and acted in a criminal fashion, then I will have to answer for my transgressions. But I have not been charged, and I have not been stripped of my rank. Events are moving fast. We need to react to them. Or would you rather the Inquisition follow the model of the High Lords and disable itself through internal politics?'

'I'm aware of current events. Can you appreciate the reasons for Inquisitor Veritus' concerns? A wrong move now could doom the Imperium.'

'Agreed. That is why I am here. Have you examined Terra's tactical situation lately? Now by your leave, Castellan, we will proceed. I have work to do.'

'You're presuming a lot,' said Kober, but he stepped to one side.

'I have to.' She walked forward, Rendenstein following. The auspex array of the doors recognised her identity and standing, and they opened before her.

The Inquisitorial Fortress made use of the caverns below the polar ice cap, but it transcended them. The honour of the Inquisition demanded more than a network of underground chambers. The Fortress' construction had seen the excavation of grandiose spaces, some larger than a grand cruiser. In them had risen walls and spires and turrets, and the greatest towers rose through the continental crust. From the surface, they resembled another glacier-cloaked mountain chain. Some of them did rise through hollowed-out peaks, while others were peaks in their own right. Prison and mailed fist, sanctuary and labyrinth, the fortress turned secrecy and power into the architecture of stone and metal.

Beyond the doors, a vaulted corridor, short and wide, led to a great rotunda. The space was ten levels high. Primary passageways, many of them served by light maglev transport, opened off the levels towards all the wings of the Fortress. The rotunda's roof was a dome. At its centre, a silver skull looked down in judgement. Its omniscience was represented in radiant lines, and the background of the dome was a pict feed of the sky above the Fortress. The effect was of standing outside, beneath the void, exposed before the gaze of the Emperor.

Inquisitors, serfs and servitors moved along all the stages. More than a few of Wienand's peers stopped to look over the balcony at her arrival. A few nodded. Others just moved on. There was a lot of traffic on the fifth level, heading east towards the Iron Watch.

Wienand heard Kober's footsteps behind her. She and Rendenstein stopped to wait. Wienand gestured to the activity on the fifth level. 'I imagine I'm the cause.'

Kober nodded. 'You know what has to happen now.'

'I would have demanded it.'

'One thing I will never question, Inquisitor Wienand, is your honour.'

'Thank you.' She quieted Rendenstein with a look.

'With your permission?' Kober asked, moving their interaction to the safe ground of formality. When Wienand made a slight bow, he led the way forward.

Stairs spiralling up the rotunda's perimeter took them to the fifth level. From there, they travelled by maglev. The train was an open set of steel pews mounted on a simple platform. It took an hour to reach the Iron Watch, and another hour still before they stood outside the entrance to the Camera Stellata. Kober stopped, and Wienand preceded him inside.

The Camera Stellata was the Octagon writ large, with a full complement of suppressive wards and psychic field dampeners. It was the site of great conclaves, but more than free debate took place here. Condemnation, punishment and execution were the possible, and frequent, outcomes of the deliberations.

The Octagon's shape emphasised the equality of the participants. Its centre was empty, so the focus moved from point to point with the currents of the debate. The Camera Stellata had a centre. Wienand walked along a black marble walkway and took her place where it ended, at a lectern mounted on a circular dais. The lectern was cast in bronze, its stand was the withered body of an enemy of the Imperium, bent beneath the weight of the accusation brought down by the winged skull that formed the lectern's top. Standing there, Wienand was orator and accused.

The chamber was a great sphere. The lectern's dais was suspended in the centre of the space. It was ringed by tiers of seats mounted into the walls. Those above the lectern were reserved for the senior inquisitors.

She turned to face her judges. 'Good. We're all here. We know the situation. We are out of time. The High Lords' greatest folly yet is under way as we speak. Do any of us expect that venture to end in anything other than disaster?' She shook her head, establishing the question as rhetorical. 'We can now count off the hours before Terra is bereft of most of its Astra Militarum defence to go along with the absence of the Navy.' She took a breath. 'I have never underestimated the threat the Ruinous Powers present to the Imperium. I won't start now. But I also know how to recognise a danger that is immediate. Fellow inquisitors, the orks are here. Now. It is clear to me, as I'm sure it is to you, that we have been left with only one option as a response. I won't insult you by trying to convince you of its necessity, because there is nothing else left to do. So I am invoking that measure now, officially, before you all.' She turned around, sweeping the assembly with her gaze. 'So,' she said. 'We have work to do.'

And she walked out.

Rendenstein was waiting outside the entrance. Her eyebrows were up. 'So that's how it's done,' she said. She had to raise her voice to be heard over the uproar that followed Wienand's exit.

'Authority derives a lot from perception,' Wienand said. 'So I used it.' She headed down the passage towards the maglev transport. Her next stop was in another wing of the Fortress, and many levels down. She tried not to think about how much distance the Armada would have covered before she could even reach Somnum Hall.

'We won't be stopped?'

'If we are, we are. If we're not, we're already wasting time.'

While they waited for the train to return to the Camera Stellata's stop, Wienand thought Rendenstein looked troubled. 'What is it?' she asked.

'After you went in, the Castellan relayed some information.'

'Something you were supposed to pass on to me?'

'He seemed to want me to know it. I don't think he cared what I did with the data. It's part of the latest briefing to have gone Fortress-wide.'

The train arrived. They boarded. They were the only passengers on this leg.

'So?' Wienand asked.

'Intercepts from a Black Templar action in the Ostrom System. The intelligence is sketchy, but it appears an ork star fortress has attacked a system in the vicinity of the Eye of Terror.'

Wienand absorbed this. 'Kober believes they've opened up a second front?'

'Yes. That the forces of Chaos are now involved.'

'Well,' Wienand said. 'Well.' She nodded to herself. 'That will be next, then.'

'What will be?'

'That concern, in whatever form it takes.'

'I see.'

The train slowed as it neared a junction with another large corridor. Inquisitors waited. They'll stop me or they won't, Wienand thought. 'Tell me what's bothering you,' she told Rendenstein. She wanted nothing unsaid between them if things went wrong in the next few seconds.

'If the Ruinous Powers are part of this war...'

Wienand finished the thought for her. 'Is Veritus right after all?'

The train came to a stop. The inquisitors boarded. A number of them had servo-skulls in attendance. These hovered low on the benches beside their controllers, recording muttered dictation as the train picked up speed again. Wienand recognised one of the new arrivals, Miliza Balduin. Wienand had met her during a joint investigation on Antagonis. She was inflexible, but fair-minded. The inflexibility meant she was a bad politician, and Wienand suspected this was why she wielded less influence than her age should have brought her. She sat in the bench ahead of Wienand and Rendenstein, then turned to appraise Wienand with a flat stare.

'Well, prodigal,' she said. 'You're here to stir us to desperate measures, are you?'

'I am. Are the deliberations over?'

Balduin shook her head. 'Not formally. But there's no doubt how they'll end. The word is out. The orks have won you the day.'

'You'll be assisting, then?'

'No. Other duties. You'll have all the help you need, I'm sure.' She began to face forward again, caught herself, and said, 'You'd better be right.'

'I am.' Wienand looked at Rendenstein. The other woman was stoic in her concern. 'Really,' Wienand told her. 'There isn't a choice.'

'I wouldn't question–'

'Yes, you would, and you do. With my thanks.'

'The risks...'

'I know them.'

'If this goes wrong...'

'I know what you're thinking. I'm not discounting Kober's information. We have to ignore it, though. It's a distraction.'

'I've never thought of Chaos as a distraction.'

'It is now.'

FIFTEEN

Sol System

'We can't have surprised them,' Kondos said.

'Of course not.' Narkissos wasn't sitting in the bridge's command throne. He paced back and forth before the primary oculus. The ork moon was filling more and more of the sky as the Armada drew closer. Its details resolved into mountain ranges and canyons of metal. There was no organisation that Narkissos could see. It was stone and iron come together as if brute force had a geology. It waited in the void for the human ships, silent and dark. There was no response. It was as still as it had been since the moment of its arrival. Narkissos entertained the crazy hope that the orks had somehow destroyed themselves in their journey, then dismissed it.

'Why aren't they attacking?' Kondos muttered. She stood midway between the throne and the helm, leaning against the cargo monitoring station as if she were contemplating leaping forward ahead of the bow.

The oculus' field of vision was crowded with ships.

Narkissos had the impression of an endless rain of metal directed at the orks. Aft of the *Militant Fire*, there was an even larger portion of the fleet. He had ordered Rallis to take the ship to the leading quarter of the Armada. He wanted to see what happened from the start.

So he told himself.

Hoping to get it all over with right away?

So he asked himself.

No, he answered. We're going to fight to live and to win.

The *Fire* was following the great bulk of the mass conveyor *Expanse of Destiny*. The huge ship, carrying a hundred thousand troops and volunteers, was just slightly to port. It seemed large and solid as a planet. It would be the *Fire*'s shield. Narkissos felt no shame in his tactic. His duty was to reach the star fortress. He wasn't Guard, and he wasn't Navy. He would leave the debates about honour to them.

So far, though, his ship hadn't needed the shield. The Armada had covered over half the distance to the ork moon. There was no response.

And then there was.

Time split, broken in half by a single moment. On the lost side, there was the calm in the void, and the grand illusion of the Proletarian Crusade in its purest, most realised form. On the other side, in the present that now unfolded with merciless revelation, was reality, and, at last, the orks took action.

At last. Narkissos realised that some part of him did respond as if something long anticipated was finally coming to pass. The knowledge made him ill. What have they done to us? he wondered.

Gaps opened on the surface of the planetoid, a sudden

spread of disease. They lit up with the fire of an endless stream of launches. The orks reached out for the Armada.

'Take us behind the *Expanse of Destiny*,' Narkissos told Rallis.

The helmsman was already changing course, putting the moon into eclipse.

'Those aren't rockets,' Kondos said.

The orks were sending squadron upon squadron of fighters. Some flew straight at the fleet. Others swung wide. They attacked the Merchants' Armada from every direction, like a grasping talon. From the other side of the moon came two large ork cruisers. They followed the fighters more slowly, and though they were dwarfed by the moon, their aggressive, brutal lines, their massive armour and their arrays of guns made their approach terrible. Narkissos became acutely aware of the lack of any fighting ship in the Armada. How had he ever believed even a single ship would get through?

Evasion wasn't going to help.

It was also the only defence he had.

'Get us in tight,' he said.

'The conveyor's engines...' Rallis said.

'Yes, I know. As close as you can to their wash.' They would hide in the nova-glare of the *Expanse*'s propulsion.

'And if the orks target the engines?' Kondos asked.

'We run.'

The ork fighters fell on the fleet. The space between the Terran ships was filled with a swarm of aggression. Multiple squadrons surrounded the bigger ships. They gathered around the *Expanse of Destiny* like flies to carrion.

The coherence of the fleet unravelled as the Terran ships responded to the attack. The movements looked more like a dance than combat. The Armada had no guns, and the orks did not fire.

'Why aren't they shooting?' Narkissos wondered.

'They're going to board,' said Kondos.

She was right. The ork fighters were larger than single-pilot ships. Narkissos had thought their bulging hulls contained bombs or torpedoes. Now he wished they did. The swarming craft around the conveyor attached themselves to its flanks. The glare from the engines hid what happened next from him.

'Can you get us any closer?' he asked Rallis.

'Risky, sir.'

'So is being cut open by the greenskins.'

Warning runes began lighting along the bridge's control surfaces. A proximity tocsin sounded. Rallis shut it off. The conveyor's engine flare grew brighter. The battle lost distinction. Its events became more distant.

The starboard-facing oculus flashed as three ork ships opened fire on a small yacht. The ship could only carry five passengers, but even its owner had stepped forward to play a part in the great adventure. It was the first ship to die, its cargo the first casualties. It was too small, Narkissos thought. It wasn't worth boarding. So the orks cleared it out of the way.

'If we're boarded...' Rallis began. He hesitated.

'What are you asking?' Narkissos could guess.

'We're faster than the conveyor. I can take us all the way in. It will be quick.'

'No,' said Kondos. 'We fight.'

'Until they take the bridge,' Narkissos said. He was already choosing his preferred defeat.

The hull of the *Expanse of Destiny* was shaking. Colonel Erich Lanser knew the sound. Breach points. He looked at his command: multiple squads of his Granite Myrmidons surrounded by a sea of volunteers. The civilians were holding weapons. At least there was that. But they were also terrified. The Crusade of their imaginations had not encompassed the possibility of fighting orks before reaching the moon.

'Rifles forward!' He stood on a raised level at the rear of the cargo bay, where he could be heard and seen. The vibration of the hull grew worse, but he couldn't tell where the break would come. 'There are thousands of us. Nothing can get in without being shot!'

He wasn't lying. What he didn't say was how little that might matter. Sergeants Bessler and Parten, closest to his position, gave him significant grins. They knew. The irony was, the regiment's last action had been against the greenskins. It had been just another suppression exercise on the Eastern Fringe, and it was the Myrmidons who had been boarding the orks, taking apart a ramshackle raiding fleet. The fight had been one-sided. Just like this one.

There was no strategy possible. There had been no time to train the civilians in much beyond how to pull a trigger. So be it. The principle, after all, was to overwhelm the orks with numbers. They could do that here too. How many troops could the orks send in at one time?

The sound of the attack became a monstrous grinding. The ork ships were using something with a blade to cut through the *Expanse of Destiny*'s shell. The noise filled the cargo bay. Lanser felt the blood drain from his face. He wasn't just hearing the vibration of attacks all along the hull. Many of them were on this section alone.

Too close together for even the most reckless boarding parties. They couldn't know if there were bulkheads sealing off one breach from another.

But if they didn't care...

The orks weren't breaching this section of the hull. They were removing it.

Lanser whirled. He ran to the rear wall, to the central interior bay door. He slammed his palm against its controls. The door groaned upwards.

'Out!' Lanser shouted. 'Now!'

The grinding scream of tearing metal drowned him out. Bessler and Parten saw him, though, and pushed the troops and volunteers near them towards the exit. Movement in the right direction began, sluggish, far too slow, then picking up speed as more people saw him gesture, and saw the beginnings of flight.

The terror-stricken noise of the assault spurred them on.

The corridor on the other side of the door was wide, large enough for the servitor-operated loaders to travel to and from the bays. The crowd ran past Lanser in a steady stream, the bottleneck minimal.

Too little, he knew. Much, much too late.

Hundreds had reached the corridor. There were thousands still in the hold. The civilians were panicking now.

Nearest the outer hull, Lanser could see Myrmidons still holding position, still training their guns in the enemy's direction. The gestures were symbolic. There would be nothing to shoot. There would be no evacuation for them, either. There wasn't time. So they stood their ground, choosing honour over pointless flight. Some looked back at Lanser over the vast space of the hold. He saluted them.

A monstrous serpent hissed.

Lanser hit the controls again and threw himself into the crush out of the bay. A great wind began to blow in from the corridor. The grind reached a peak of agony. Then there was a pop that was larger than sound. Almost half the bay's wall vanished. Slabs of the ship's hull spun away. The atmosphere blasted out into the void. It scooped up the Crusaders in the hold and scattered them into the great and cold nothing. Two ork fighters hung in the opening. Articulated arms extended from their noses, wielding circular saws four metres in diameter. They were spinning, but the grind was gone. There was only the blank roar of the wind.

The force of the venting pulled at Lanser like chains. Blood burst from his nose and ears. The door was halfway down. He pushed against the hurricane of decompression. He gripped the side of the doorway and lunged forward, shoving against struggling backs. The man in front of him fell. He banged into Lanser as the wind took him back. Lanser clutched the doorway harder. The yank tried to dislocate his arm.

The door was less than two metres from being closed. The roar became a desperate, whistling shriek. Lanser ducked low and hauled himself around the corner, into the corridor.

He slammed the top of his head against the descending barrier and collapsed against the wall. The door closed, trapping a handful of Crusaders beneath it. The wind's shriek continued a few seconds longer as flesh and bone held back heavy steel for a moment more. Then the pressure of the mechanism and the weight of the door won, severing and crushing.

The wind died. Lungs rasping, Lanser stood. He moved forward to take the lead of the column of Crusaders who had managed to reach the corridor. He pushed past perhaps three hundred civilians before he reached Bessler and Parten's squads. They were the only Myrmidons who had made it.

'Doesn't make sense,' Parten said. She wiped a smear of blood from her upper lip. 'Why go to the trouble of peeling the ship open? Why not just torpedo it if they're not going to board?'

'Because it amuses them?' Bessler suggested.

Lanser shook his head. 'I've never known greenskins to entertain themselves by taking a slower approach to violence.' He shouted for silence. The sobs of the civilians quieted enough for him to hear what he had feared: more of the vibrating grind coming from elsewhere in the ship. 'They are boarding,' he said. 'That was a decapitation move. They took out most of the opposition we could muster at a stroke.'

'Which means they knew what they were doing,' Parten said, awed.

'I'm not interested in what they planned,' said Lanser before Parten could continue. The implications of orks taking the time to attack a ship based on its layout and probable complement of defenders did not need airing. That talk would not help with what needed to be done, and would change nothing.

So what do we do? He thought of the *Expanse of Destiny*'s other cargo bays, holding tens of thousands more Crusaders. They orks had likely vented them too. 'We stick to the interior passageways,' he said. 'Make for the bridge. If they are boarding, that's where we'll have to hold them.'

He looked back at the civilians. Many still looked determined. All were terrified. The dream of the Crusade had soured.

'You wanted to fight the greenskins?' Lanser shouted to them. 'You're lucky. You're getting the chance early. Let's go tear them apart.'

He led the charge aft, towards the ship's superstructure. Parten and Bessler's troops shouted defiance, spreading the will to fight. And in the tighter confines of the corridors, three hundred souls became a crowd, a force, a surging wall of anger looking for an enemy to kill.

Deeper in the ship, the vibrations of the breaching faded. It became possible to pretend that nothing was happening. Lanser sensed the confidence of the Crusaders build still more.

Two-thirds of the way to the bridge, they found the enemy. About twenty orks burst out of a side passage linking to one of the smaller cargo holds. Lanser had no chance to give orders. He and the Myrmidons dropped into crouches and started firing at the intersection ahead. The first ranks of the civilians fired too. There was no discipline to the volleys of

las, but there was no way to miss, either. Orks went down. The humans cheered triumph and rage, loud enough to shake the walls of the passageway.

The orks didn't return fire. They barrelled down the hall towards the Crusaders. A few more fell. Then Lanser drew his sword and ran forward. He couldn't let the orks steal the momentum. The Crusaders charged with him.

The two forces collided. The humans had the numbers. The orks had the physical strength. The battle became a melee, a riot of blades and blood. The Crusaders' arsenal was basic: lasguns and bayonets. Few had any armour. The orks all carried guns, but waded in with their own blades.

Lanser had fought the greenskins before. He was used to seeing their huge machetes and axes, but he had never felt his own weapons outclassed by the brutes' armament. The weapons these orks wielded, and the forms of armour they wore, were as massive as ever, but it seemed that their exuberant brutality was the product of skill rather than crude overcompensation. Imperial blades dulled and bent against orkish plate. Imperial bodies came apart beneath orkish blows.

The floor was awash with blood. Lanser could barely move, caught in the crush of struggling human and greenskin bodies. The density of the struggle helped. The orks were crowded in as much as he was, and denied the leverage to use their greater strength to its full effect. He slipped his sword beneath the helmet of one beast. He drove the point up through the ork's chin and into its brain. The press of bodies held the corpse upright long enough for him to withdraw the blade.

A taller ork made a noise that was snarl and laugh. It swung its cleaver at him. He couldn't duck. He tilted his head to the side. It was enough. The blade sank into the side of the skull of the man behind him, chopping through at eye level. Lanser raised his laspistol and shot the ork in the centre of the forehead. The beast blinked, its skin smouldering with las burn. It pulled its arm back to strike again, knocking its smaller kin aside with the force of the gesture. Lanser fired again, five more times. He had to sear the ork's face to slag before the monster finally dropped.

Lanser took half a step forward, walking on bodies. A huge fist struck him in the temple. Stunned, vision bleary, he lunged forward, sword extended. Luck or the Emperor's hand guided his blow. The impact of the blade sinking through greenskin muscle to the heart almost dislocated his arm.

The orks kept coming. There was no forcing them back. They advanced, a battering ram of flesh that hit like stone and broke the human wall down. Step by step, the Crusaders were forced back down the hall. But they fought and they stabbed with last-chance desperation. They died by the dozens. The orks died one by one.

The numbers won.

Drenched in gore, Lanser leaned against the wall. He gasped for breath. His right side ached from a power claw hit. If the ork had been able to do more than glance him, he would have been crushed. As it was, he could feel the movement of broken ribs. He wondered how long it would be before a floating bone punctured a lung. He pushed away thoughts of a medicae bay. He didn't have the luxury of that hope. He would be lucky to live long enough to die from this wound.

The corridor had become a slaughterhouse. The corpses of orks and humans lay in a mire of blood. Most of the ork bodies were still intact. Many of the humans were scattered remains. The stench was thick. Lanser felt like he was breathing blood and offal. Parten was as blood-soaked as he was, but none of her wounds were life-threatening. Bessler's left arm had been crushed to jelly below the elbow. One of his troopers was applying a tourniquet to his stump. He was pale, barely keeping unconsciousness at bay. Both squads had been decimated. Two-thirds of the civilians had been killed. But they had won. The survivors' eyes were wide with the dulled drunkenness of their victory.

Lanser pushed himself away from the wall.

'Keep going,' he called out, voice rasping. If they stopped to rest, they would lose the momentum of this hard triumph. Despair was one bad thought away. He started to walk, stumbled. He stopped, aware of the eyes on him, straightened, and when he was sure of his footing, started forward again. His gait was stronger. He wasn't going to fall.

Ragged now, battered, slower, but desperate to fight because that was all they had left, Myrmidons and Crusaders headed for the bridge. Lanser kept hearing the sounds of combat, but they were always distant echoes, travelling through mazes of passageways to reach him. Whatever was happening, it was too far away for him to bring help. The bridge remained the goal.

Parten moved forward to join him. 'Permission to ask a question, colonel?'

'Go ahead, sergeant.'

'How long can we hold them at the bridge?'

'We'll seal the door. Even when they breach it, the entrance is narrower than this corridor. I've seen it. That will create a bottleneck for them, an edge for us. We don't have to defeat them here. Just hold them back long enough.'

'For what?'

'For us to reach the moon.' He said it as if that would be the end of things. It will be, he thought.

She nodded, believing in his optimism or accepting their fate.

They climbed the levels from the cargo decks, up towards the bridge at the top of the superstructure. The echoes of battle became more distant. Maybe there was time, Lanser thought. Maybe they had pulled ahead of the ork boarding parties enough to establish something like a real defence.

At the base of the plain metal staircase leading to the bridge, he could hear activity from above. Purposeful, but not violent. That gave him hope. He ran up the stairs, his breath tearing into his lungs with a knife. The stairs ended in a wide passage leading port and starboard, with the doors to the bridge straight ahead.

There was blood on the deck. It seeped from the open doorway to the bridge; the orks were already here. The battle was over. The orks' debased slave-race were hauling out the corpses of the crew and tossing them in piles lining the corridor walls. They glanced at Lanser. They snickered, then called out to their masters as they scampered back onto the bridge.

Lanser moved forward. He couldn't feel his legs. He

couldn't feel his arms, either. His body was a collection of disjointed fragments, all acting independently, all moving forward with no purpose. His brain was numb. He was a servitor, completing a hopeless task because there was nothing else to do.

His left arm raised his pistol. His fingers were clumsy. It was hard to fire. His right arm hung limp, dragging the point of his sword over the decking.

Noises behind him now. Cries, wails, the thudding of boots. Was that the whine of las-fire? Maybe. He didn't care. It didn't matter. It was so far away.

An ork warboss emerged from the bridge a giant that had to bend in half to fit under the doorway. The deck shook beneath its armoured feet. It looked like a tank that had learned to walk. When Lanser shot it, its lips parted in a smile, showing fangs the length of his hand, its eyes amused. When it backhanded him, shattering his skeleton and sending him flying back down the staircase, the gesture was casual, maybe even disappointed.

Maybe even bored.

The *Expanse of Destiny* pulled up. Its nose tilted towards the ork cruiser riding above the cloud of the Armada. The movement was emphatic and slow, a glacier with delusions of ramming. Narkissos was about to order Rallis to stay in its wake when he saw the ork fighters moving away, heading for other targets. The *Expanse* was not attempting a suicidal attack, he realised. She was already lost. Her new masters were taking the ship out of formation to join with the cruiser.

There was no shelter here now.

The irony of worrying about shelter, given his ship's destination, passed through his mind for the length of time it took him to draw a breath. 'Helmsman,' he said to Rallis, 'no more hiding. Time to run. Full power.'

'There are other big ships,' Kondos said.

'They won't be ours long, not at this rate.'

'Exactly. Look.'

He always paid attention when Kondos made that request. Their shared gifts were the reason the *Militant Fire* had survived to see this day. He was the improviser. She saw the big picture. She took in the myriad variables of a situation, creating the map for Narkissos to navigate.

So he focused on the big ships. The ork squadrons were thick around them, tearing them open and inserting boarding parties. Away from the giants, the smaller ships were falling prey. Many were boarded. The smallest were destroyed. But the ones closest to the mass conveyors and factory ships were being ignored as the orks concentrated on the big prizes.

'Port,' Narkissos said. 'Down thirty degrees. The *Europa Forge*.'

'Behind the engines?' Rallis asked, already making the course correction.

'No. Keep up the speed.' Beneath his feet, Narkissos could just detect the faint vibration in the deck as the *Militant Fire* powered up. She was ready to race for her life, for the lives of all aboard, and for the life of any hope of victory. 'Skim by her. Then the *Spreading Word*.' He pointed to the colony ship just beyond the *Europa Forge*. 'Understand?'

'I do.'

'We have a fast ship, helmsman. Let's prove it to the orks.'

'They won't even see us.'

'That's the whole idea,' said Kondos.

The *Militant Fire* streaked towards the *Europa Forge*. 'Like a stone over water,' Narkissos urged, and Rallis took him at his word. He took the ship in at a low angle of approach, as if he might really land on the other vessel's refinery. He passed over the superstructure. The orks were clustered on the flanks of the hull. For a moment, the run looked clear, but then another squadron appeared off the prow, heading straight for the bridge. The *Fire* was flying level with them.

'Down!' Narkissos yelled.

A few decades earlier, Rallis would have questioned such a reckless order. Once, in the early days of the helmsman's service, Narkissos had forced him at gunpoint to perform a manoeuvre that Rallis had maintained would tear the ship apart. It hadn't, and they had escaped faster, more agile raiders. Rallis no longer questioned him. He plunged into the insane as if he were piloting a fighter, not a cargo ship.

Rallis dropped the nose. The *Militant Fire* arrowed at the refinery. A collision could take out a large part of the fleet if the smaller ship punched through the plasma containment tanks.

The surface of the reservoirs came closer. The *Fire* was below the height of the chimney vents. They rose like a steel forest on either side. Narkissos felt the vertigo of rushing disaster, but he said nothing. He sensed Rallis' need to pull up, but the helmsman maintained course.

Another second. Then another. The orks passing overhead. *Wait. Wait.* The impact in two breaths. *Now.*

'Level us!'

One breath. The perspective of the oculus changed with tectonic lethargy. The second and last breath... The *Militant Fire* flew straight. The struts of the belly auspex array snapped off as they brushed against the *Europa Forge*'s reservoir. Ahead, the ship bulked upwards. The orks were now behind. 'Up,' Narkissos ordered at the same moment Rallis altered the course again. They pulled away from the *Europa Forge*. Rallis held them in a close parallel flight with it until they passed over the bow. Then he angled towards the *Spreading Word*.

Any form of order in the Merchants' Armada had collapsed. The fleet was a storm of ships, boiling with evasions and captures. Collisions killed more vessels than the orks as panicked flights intersected. The *Militant Fire* flew through a dissipating fog of plasma. Fragments of wreckage tumbled by. As she closed with the *Spreading Word*, she encountered what Narkissos thought was another debris cloud. The remains were corpses, thousands of Crusaders, frozen in their last agony, sucked out of the open flanks of the colony ship.

For every ship that destroyed another, and for every one that was boarded, there were two that kept running. The fleet was a confusion of movement, but it still closed with the ork moon. Some of its elements raced far ahead of the others. The distance between ships grew. The sense of a collective action disintegrated, but there were so many vessels that there was still a crowd, still a mass migration of humans towards the fortress.

Closer yet. Narkissos had to guard against the temptation to gaze at the moon's gorgon image and lose the thread of the moment-by-moment decisions needed to see the *Militant Fire* to its destination. He was sweating. He was frightened. His ship's path was crossed again and again by squadrons of brutal predators. On all sides, the heroes of the Proletarian Crusade were dying, killed on boarded ships, ejected into the void, or vaporised by collisions. But he was also exhilarated because the *Fire* was not alone in its race. There was more than terror, flight and destruction visible in the oculus. There was also determination. There was strength. There were no more ork fighters emerging from the star fortress. For the first time, Narkissos dared imagine that their resources were not infinite.

The strategy that Speaker Tull had conceived was working. The Imperium had turned the orks' own tactics against them. 'We're going to do it,' Narkissos said, turning hope into words. 'We're going to flood them with our numbers.' What he said was an incantation, an attempt at a great alchemy: hope into words, words into reality.

'Port, upper quadrant,' Kondos said.

Narkissos looked. 'Are you serious?' Kondos had indicated one of the ork cruisers. The *Militant Fire* was ahead of almost all the large ships now. Most of the Imperial vessels in its company were smaller than it was.

'Why not?' Kondos asked. 'Aren't we trying to get close to the greenskins?'

Narkissos grinned. 'Yes, we are.' There were very few ork fighters near the cruiser. The big ship was doing little beyond being a massive escort, protecting the squadrons against non-existent Imperial fire. 'Helmsman, let's embrace the madness.'

He imagined he could actually hear the blood drain from the faces of the bridge crew. He laughed. It was that or let terror close his throat altogether. Rallis muttered prayers under his breath, but turned the *Fire*'s nose towards the ork monster. They closed the distance quickly. They shot past a handful of ork fighters, which ignored them. Narkissos wondered what the greenskins thought when they saw his ship's trajectory. Could orks be stunned by the lunacy of an adversary? It pleased him to think so.

The thought that the orks just ignored the ship pleased him less, because behind it lurked the question of why they would not care.

The *Militant Fire* flew beneath the cruiser's hull. Narkissos had a sense of metal dense as muscle, large as a city. The cruiser was a hellish god that could annihilate his ship with as little notice as he would swat an insect.

His shoulders hunched, as if the image alone of the ork vessel could crush him. But then they left it behind too.

And now there was only the moon. The dark divinity of the cruiser faded to nothing. The star fortress filled the oculus. Narkissos confronted an entire world built for war. The monstrosity became all that was real, and it was a reality that was shaped to enact a greater monster's will. It was a reality that travelled.

There was too much impossible in his vision. Too much horror. In defence of his sanity, he narrowed his focus to the geography, to the purpose of landing his ship where there was no space port. He concentrated on what he knew would be the last act of his career.

Tunnel vision. He saw mountains, and he tuned out their constructed nature. He looked for a plain. He clutched the dream of victory. It held reality at bay.

Fuelled by the dream, followed by hundreds more dreaming vessels, the *Militant Fire* brought Juskina Tull's vision to the orks.

SIXTEEN

The ork moon

The moon had an atmosphere. The air was foul, ashy, reeking of burning gases and the effluvium of xenos industry. It was thin. When the *Militant Fire*'s cargo door opened, Haas felt the immediate urge to gasp. Yet the air was breathable, and no worse than the more toxic hives of Terra, except for the stench of the inhuman. The smell was acrid, a mixture of filthy industry and the foul organic. Though it was dry, it had the cloying grip of high humidity. Above all, it was an odour that she had never encountered before, and she bristled, a hunted animal reacting to the approach of the predator. The air had a taste, too. Haas wanted to spit. Her mouth was full of iron, promethium and rotten blood.

The wind had a hollow, rasping sound, a snarl echoing through organ pipes.

An atmosphere. The orks had given their artificial planetoid a *surface* atmosphere. There was no reason for them to do so. The outside of the star fortress showed no sign of life. The greenskins had performed a gigantic technological feat, it seemed, simply because they *could*. That excess of power was daunting.

The surface visible from the ship was pockmarked rock, with no dust. The patchwork quality of the planetoid extended even to what had appeared from orbit to be natural formations. The orks had done more than carve an existing moon into the canyons and mountain ranges that suited them or raise barriers thousands of metres high and hundreds of kilometres long. Haas had the disturbing impression that they had assembled the fortress out of the pieces of other moons. They had created a world out of nothing.

How can we defeat an enemy that powerful?

Through their mistakes.

Kord refused to disembark. He hung back at the rear as the civilians and Imperial Guard descended the ramp. He walked slowly, and when he reached the door, he stopped.

'What are you doing?' Haas demanded. She had joined him for the landing out of consideration of their partnership on Terra, but her patience was exhausted. The man who had talked up the Crusade had become a shameful specimen.

Kord stared at the expanse of the ork moon before them. 'I can't,' he said.

'Get down or I'll shoot you myself.'

'No,' said a third voice. 'You will not.'

She turned around. The last of the Astra Militarum contingents to disembark were the Jupiter Storm. Commissar Sever had come up behind them. 'You are under military command now,' he said. 'That decision is not yours.'

'I understand,' Haas said. She stepped to one side.

Sever regarded Kord with a cold, absolute contempt. 'Disembark,' he said.

Kord spread his hands, pleading. 'I–' he began.

Sever pulled his bolt pistol out of its holster and shot Kord in the left eye. The Arbitrator's skull exploded. Blood splashed Haas' armour.

Sever turned to her.

'Thank you, commissar,' Haas said, 'for preserving the honour of the Adeptus Arbites.'

She followed the Jupiter Storm out of the *Militant Fire*.

'They got greedy,' said Captain Fernau of the Orion Watch. 'They made a mistake.' His laugh was relieved. 'So they *can* make mistakes.'

Gattan grunted. He wanted to believe Fernau. He didn't dare. He had to take the realities of the battlefield as they unfolded, not as he would wish them to be. 'We'll see,' he said.

Fernau took in the deployment with a wide sweep of his arm. 'We are seeing.'

They were standing on the upper hull of the *Militant Fire*. They had a view of the plain where the ships had come down, and of the mustering of the army.

The plain was fifty kilometres wide, bracketed by mountain chains that lost height as they converged to the south. That meeting point, fifteen kilometres away, was the target. During the descent, several ships had observed what looked like a massive gate closing. The Crusade needed a way inside the fortress, and the plain's size and proximity to the goal made it a suitable starting point.

Maybe Fernau was right, Gattan thought. The orks had taken many of the larger ships, but they had not sent out anything close to enough fighters to stop the Armada. Hundreds more vessels had made it through. By lighter, by shuttle, and by ships that would never take off again, legions of Crusaders had put boots to soil. Thousands, then hundreds of thousands, and now millions. Gattan had never been part of an operation on this scale. A sea of warriors hungry for greenskin blood stretching back as far as he could see on land flat as sheet metal. The sight made the toll the orks had exacted seem insignificant. This was a triumph. Wasn't it?

Fernau thought so. Gattan was uneasy. There were enough companies of Astra Militarum left for some kind of coordination, but the losses *had* been great. Though the banners of the Jupiter Storm, Granite Myrmidons, Orion Watch, Auroran Rifles and the Eagles of Nazca were raised high, and the uniforms of each regiment were beyond counting, the vast majority of those uniforms were worn by civilians. Most of the heavy armour had been captured. All the senior officers had been aboard the big ships. There was no one ranking higher than captain on the ground.

At least they'd been able to establish vox-communication with each other even as they were landing. And the broad lines of the strategy had been established before the Armada had left Terra. There had been enough guidance to make the target clear. The deployment itself had to be simple. There was little to be done with the civilians except to send them marching in the right direction with instructions to shoot the enemy.

* * *

A squadron of ork bombers roared overhead. It did not attack. Neither had the few others that had overflown the landing site during the last few hours.

'What are they doing?' Gattan wondered aloud.

'Reconnaissance,' Fernau answered.

'Unusual restraint. We're a very big target.'

'Too big. Nothing flights of that size can take on.'

'So where are the others?'

Fernau shrugged. 'Not here, so no help to them. They're making more mistakes. Giving us a chance to move against them.'

Maybe. In the end, the truth didn't matter. There was only one course of action open.

Its engine growling, a Chimera pulled up beside the *Militant Fire*. Gattan clasped forearms with Fernau. 'For Terra and the Emperor,' he said.

'For Terra and the Emperor.'

Gattan climbed down onto the roof of his command vehicle. Another rumbled up behind it to collect Fernau.

The march began. The heavy armour that had reached the star fortress led the way. Over a hundred Leman Russ battle tanks in all their variants, and half that number of Chimeras and Hellhounds formed something too wide to be called a wedge. They were an advancing wall. The surface of the moon vibrated with the force of their passing. Behind them came the foot soldiers of the Proletarian Crusade. Slowly at first, but then with mounting momentum, the immense army advanced on the gates to the enemy stronghold.

* * *

Haas was in the leading elements of the attack, moving at a forced march speed behind the armour. She could see nothing ahead of her except iron and blue-black exhaust. Her ears rang with the roar of engines, but the guns were silent for now. The orks had not yet attacked.

She looked up into the sky. The Crusade was on the night side of the planetoid. She could see Terra, large in its shining majesty, small in its vulnerability. That was what she had come here to protect. As long as she could see Terra, she wouldn't mind dying in this place. The ork moon had besieged the consciousness of every soul on Terra for weeks. Now the orks were the ones besieged. That in itself was a victory. We've come this far, Haas thought, and you failed to stop us. You'll fail again.

Though her lungs laboured, her strides became stronger. She moved faster. She felt the hand of the Emperor at her back, and she gave thanks.

Though it was night, the visibility on the surface of the moon was high. To the reflected light from Terra was added a glow from the mountain ranges. They were lined with what looked like veins of molten lava. A wash of red reached across the plain.

The mountains jutted like a monster's teeth from the plain. There were no foothills, no rise of the land, no transition at all between a featureless level and the brutal vertical. The peaks could not be climbed. They were an absolute barrier. The valley between the mountain chains narrowed quickly, and Haas was close enough to the western range to see the welds on them, the seams between an infinity of overlapping metal plates, as if the orks had begun constructing a ship's hull and been unable to stop. The jagged, crooked, intersecting streams of light were not lava. They looked even more like blood flowing just beneath the iron flesh. The mix of the geological, the artificial and the organic was unnerving.

An hour into the march, a glow appeared in the distance, where the mountain chains met. It was a false sunrise in the eternal night. The light was a sullen red with irregular pulses of green.

'We have a target!' The voice over the vox-casters was Gattan's. Haas could just see him, two vehicles ahead, riding high in the open hatch of the Chimera.

The march became a charge. Haas began to run. They had overwhelmed the orks this far. They would do it again.

'They're going to open the gate,' Gattan voxed his fellow captains.

'Good,' said Fernau.

The light at the juncture of the mountain chains grew brighter. Then the clamour began. From the centre of the light came the orks. They began as a boiling disturbance in the distance. The threat gathered definition. Within minutes, Gattan could make out the figures of individual orks. Coming up the middle of the infantry were Battlewagons. As far as Gattan could tell, the human tanks outnumbered the ork vehicles. In spite of himself, he grinned in anticipation.

Closer. The mountain chains were only a kilometre apart now. The yowling celebration of the greenskins competed with the war chants of the Astra Militarum and the shouted prayers of the civilians. Gattan tried to guess the size of the ork army. Thousands, he thought. It seemed a much smaller force than the human one. The Crusaders were a solid wall across the entire width of the plain. The orks were in a narrower formation.

Closer.

'Fire!' Gattan ordered, and the other captains echoed his command.

The Leman Russ cannons opened up. A wide cluster of blasts chewed up the ork advance. The barrage battered one of the lead Battlewagons to scrap. There was a strange cleanness to the explosions. Fireballs hurled chunks of bodies skyward, but there was no dust, no rocky debris. The shells left the surface of the moon unscarred.

The orks rushed on, unfazed by their losses.

The snarls and the prayers and the chants and the cannon fire and the pounding of running feet were all one, a giant, indistinguishable cacophony of war. The gap between the two armies shrank to nothing.

Impact.

The orks hit the wall of the Imperial armour. They broke against it like foam on rocks. Gattan felt the Chimera jolt as it ran over greenskin bodies. The Hellhounds sent out a torrent of flame over the enemy. For several seconds, the mechanised Imperial advance achieved a total purge. But the orks kept coming. Faster brutes and stronger ones pushed through the spaces between the vehicles and fell on the human infantry. Gattan manned the heavy bolter, gunning down as many as he could. He couldn't get them all. Over the sound of the guns, he heard the rising wave of screams and snarls as the melee began.

Human and ork tanks fired at each other at point-blank range. Every shot hit. The vehicles of both forces disintegrated in flames and tearing metal, their deaths savaging nearby infantry. The losses mounted, but the greater human numbers made the difference. The advance slowed, but it did not stop.

'Faster!' Gattan ordered. 'Get us through!' The Chimera's armour wasn't as thick as a Leman Russ'. It had already taken one hit that would have incinerated Gattan if he hadn't ducked down the hatch the second before the shell struck. He was back up again the next instant, making himself visible to both orks and humans. Let one fear him, he thought, and the other take heart from his defiance.

Forward still, with more and more of the ork Battlewagons down. Gattan could see past them to the open gate itself. Then a huge shape emerged from the entrance. His eyes widened. 'Hard right!' he yelled. 'Evasive–'

He couldn't hear his words as the enormous gun of the ork battle fortress roared. The shell blew up a Hellhound close to Gattan's left. He turned his head away from the heat of the flames as the vehicle's ignited promethium reserves splashed outward, immolating human and ork alike.

The new ork tank was immense, four times the size of any other vehicle on the field. Its main gun looked like it belonged on a cruiser. The ork foot soldiers hooted their derision at the humans as they swarmed past their monster. The battle fortress moved forward slowly. Each shot was a high-explosive bomb, and each killed another Imperial tank. The few that missed made huge craters of human flesh in the infantry.

'Surround it!' said Gattan. 'All vehicles concentrate fire on this target!'

Clicks of acknowledgement on the vox, and Gattan had a moment to wonder when the overall leadership of the attack had fallen to him. Then there were no thoughts but the destruction of the monster. Leman Russ, Hellhound and Chimera encircled the battle fortress. Its gigantic turret moved with a sluggish laziness and picked them off one at a time. Their shells were pinpricks against its armour.

Gattan prayed that the accumulation of pinpricks would be enough.

The turret gradually moved his way. The Chimera kept circling, but the gun moved closer, each terrible blast consigning more of Terra's regiments to oblivion. Fernau's curses were cut off by a vox-squeal as his Chimera vanished.

But the miracle happened. Gattan saw cracks appear in the battle fortress' flanks. The fissures glowed red, then orange, then white. Even as he shouted to keep firing, that they were besting the monster, a terrible thought came to him.

He realised that this was too easy.

He realised too late.

The battle fortress exploded.

Haas threw herself down as the blast slammed fire and wind over both armies. The charge of the ork infantry had pushed her back even as other Crusaders, closer to the tanks, had continued to move forward. They were swallowed by the death of the battle fortress. The boom, so loud it was a physical force, echoed back and forth between the mountain chains. When it faded, all that remained of Imperial and ork armour was a coral reef of smoking, twisted metal.

Ork reinforcements came leaping over the ruins. They slammed into the stunned Crusaders like a battering ram. They smashed through the soft bodies of humans, advancing dozens of metres before the sheer volume of Crusaders slowed them down. The orks laid into the butchery with chainblades and power claws. For several seconds, the human force disintegrated further, its untrained warriors ground to pulp, their blood splashing over their comrades and killers alike, staining the ground red with the taint of folly. Many civilians broke and ran.

'Fight or die, cowards!' Sever, his uniform shredded and smoking, his face pouring blood, strode past Haas. Then he yelled, 'Now!' and ducked.

Haas did the same. So did the Crusaders whose discipline still held, who listened to orders, who understood. Dozens more were cut down by friendly fire, clearing the way for the disciplined, concentrated volleys of las from a platoon of the Jupiter Storm to cut into the ork flanks. Grenades followed. The blasts killed humans too. Needed sacrifices as the counter-attack began to eat into the ork column.

The greenskins fired back. They began to spread out. Their flank grew longer, opening up more opportunities for the Crusaders. Haas saw hers and rushed in. She drove her shock maul down on the skull of an ork that was reaching for Sever. The brute stumbled, stunned by the discharge. While it was slowed, she fired her laspistol into its eyes.

Her training was in the suppression of mobs, not military combat. But she looked at the orks as a well-armed mob, and her instincts kept her alive. In their undisciplined rampage, they reminded her of rebellious underhive gangs. But much stronger.

She took a step back as her target dropped. She hunched down, using its body as a shield. The next orks rushing forward swung without looking for her. Their blades went wide. She fired up, blinding one, then caught it in the face with the maul as it fell forward, tripping over the corpse of its fellow. Another brought its cleaver in too quickly for her to dodge. She turned her body and caught the blade in her pauldron. She rammed the shock maul into the greenskin's belly. It snarled in anger. It was too big, too powerful to stun, but it reflexively lost its grip on its blade. It reached for her throat with both hands.

She fired into its face at the same time that Sever did. She looked at the commissar just as he was struck from behind. He dropped to his knees. She fired at the ork towering over him while she lashed out blindly to either side with her shock maul, trying to stave off an ambush on herself.

There were orks on all sides. She and Sever were drowning in the green tide.

Haas' maul struck bodies, drawing grunts. Her shots didn't kill the ork over Sever. It was too big. But they drew its attention. It came for her, a colossus in spiked metal plate wielding a large hammer. Sever must have been hit by the most glancing of blows.

A hit from an ork behind her clipped Haas' helmet and struck the cleaver still embedded in her shoulder's ablative armour. The blade went deeper, drawing blood, before it fell out. She fell towards the giant, tucking herself into the tumble and rolling along the ground between the ork's legs. She spun around and fired at its back.

The las did nothing against its armour. It turned, but then there were hands pulling her and Sever out of its path, and a storm surge of Crusaders, brandishing bayonets, crashed into the monster. It roared at them, smashed heads to pulp with its hammer, but they kept coming in endless, desperate frenzy. There were so many, they climbed over each other as they struck at the ork. Haas made it to her feet. Sever was already up, exhorting the civilians who streamed by on either side, buffeting him in their rush. She witnessed the impossible: an ork submerged by the human tide.

Dozens of Crusaders died. But they trampled the ork to death.

A group of orks came back hard, avenging their leader, and the greenskin formation was diluted still further. More platoons of Imperial Guard closed in. They turned heavy weapons on the orks. Rockets and flamers exterminated unlucky humans as well, but there were fewer greenskins, and always more humans.

We're fighting like them, Haas realised, and that part of her mind that could still think critically was horrified that the children of the Emperor had reached this state. The rest of her met savagery with savagery, and she rejoiced to see the enemy's advance slowed, then stopped.

Then reversed.

Haas didn't realise, at first, that the miracle was happening. She and Sever were moving forward, acting as a coordinated pair against each foe. Forward, forward, forward, over the wreckage of the tanks, and at last it registered that they were never stepping back, and that the direction was consistent, and that they were speeding up.

The orks were retreating, and they were dying as they did so.

The Crusaders pursued. They tasted blood and victory, and the roar was unlike anything Haas had yet heard. There was all the hope and all the desperation that had fuelled the great cries of defiance on Terra. But now the enemy was before them, and the enemy was running, here, on its great machine of war that was the source of globe-spanning terror. The orks were fleeing. They could be defeated. In the name of the Emperor, they were defeated. The xenos threat that had annihilated the Imperial Fists was being routed by an army that had little more than faith and dire need behind it.

Haas joined in the shout. Her throat and her lungs were scraped raw by the air. She didn't care. She was part of the triumph. Expelling all of the awful fear of the last days, she howled her hate and feral joy. She raced after the orks, and she was part of a massive wave of humanity so powerful it must surely sweep mountains aside.

The tiny part of her consciousness that still thought tactically wondered why the reinforcing ork army had not been larger. It wondered why it had all been infantry. It wondered why there had been no tanks, no artillery and no heavy weapons of any kind.

None of these questions mattered. Not now. Not in this moment of moments.

The orks retreated faster. They put distance between themselves and the humans. Haas was frustrated not to have more greenskin blood on her hands, but she rejoiced that the enemy was so desperate to escape.

The Crusaders were close now to the light, the glow that came from underground. At the point where the ranges met, Haas could now see that immense doors had slid apart to allow the orks to come up a ramp wide enough to accommodate a dozen tanks abreast of each other. The greenskins pounded down the steep slope, and the doors began to close. They were huge, metres thick, tall as a hab-block, but set in the ground only twenty degrees from the horizontal. With the leading edge of the human wave still several hundred metres away, they began to slide closed.

So did the mountains.

The ground beneath Haas' feet shook, throwing her down. The grinding of a vast mechanism reached up through stone. And the mountains walked. The event was too great, too impossible, so that her mind refused for several seconds to accept what her eyes saw. The ranges moved towards each other with a metallic rumble that was the voice of an entire world. The moon was changing before her eyes.

Thousands of metres high, dozens of kilometres long, the barriers were coming together to form the last of all walls. The Crusaders had run into a trap that would kill millions at a stroke.

The race halted. The roar turned into screams. There was nowhere to run. The ships were too far. The mountain faces were sheer and high. There was time only for the fullness of terror to take hold.

'Go!' Sever yelled. 'Deny them this victory!'

Only Haas heard him.

She ran for the doors. There was still an opening several metres wide. It shrank at an unhurried pace. It still might be too fast, because the shaking of the ground was so intense, she couldn't run in a straight line.

Haas looked at nothing but her goal. The world was closing in on both sides of her. There was no sound except the apocalypse rumble of metal and stone. There was also no one in front of her. She had the lead.

She pushed all thought away. She banished hope. She ignored the pain in her lungs and her legs. She became a thing of one movement alone. If there were other runners near her, she didn't know. They didn't matter. Her flight mattered. The mountains mattered. Nothing else.

Adrenaline gave her wings. The limits of the human body clipped them. She was slowing down, a dozen metres from the end of the line, and the doors had almost shut. But something was happening behind her. A new sound had begun, almost as loud as the rumble. It was a sound that was wet, and cracked. The air became thick, coppery, moist.

A few more steps, her legs stumping like rotten logs. Was she still running? It seemed she was crawling. And a river of blood, foaming, torrential, rushed ahead of her. It lapped at the doors as if it would quench their thirst. The mountains were less than ten metres apart. She could see both sides in her peripheral vision. The edges of the world closed in. The entrance shrank. She wouldn't make it. She was too far.

Grind and rumble and screams torn apart by the edges of splintering bones. The sound of an ocean snapping into shards. The blood surged. Torrent became deluge, became tidal wave. It lifted her up. She tumbled in the flow, gagging and choking. Her vision became a whirl of jagged horrors, the darkness of the blood tide giving way to the momentary sight of what lay behind, of the climbing swell of bodies rising to the heavens, millions of people fused into a mass of broken dolls. A flash of Sever disappearing beneath the blood. Up and down, over and over, tossed by the pressurised current, battered by the flotsam of bones. She lost her weapons. She tried to swim, but she was an insect in the clutches of the moon's fist. Drowning, soul blasted by the hell-vision, she had no thoughts, no hope, no awareness at all. She had only her last instinct, the bodily drive to struggle, even when all point had been lost.

The world was nightmare. The world was speed and pain and the warm choking in her lungs and the towering shadows finally meeting. She hit something very large and solid. She started to black out. Then she was moving down, and still down, and the violence of the torrent faded.

Behind and above, a great, final, echoing boom. The blood released her.

She gagged, vomited blood. She wiped the gore from her eyes. She was lying on a slope, surrounded by red light pulsing green. On either side were moving pistons like great towers, gears the size of cathedrals. Below, she heard the stir of an uncountable army, of a strength in weapons and ships that denied all measure.

She was inside the moon.

Narkissos and Kondos watched the mountains come together from the ramp leading to the *Militant Fire*'s primary cargo bay. Narkissos felt a jolt up his spine, and realised he had sat down. His legs refused to hold him. Kondos remained standing, motionless, as if the sight had turned her to stone.

In the first seconds of the trap's activation, Narkissos had thought the chains in their entirety were moving. They were not. The orks had constructed them in sections. Only the region of the plain where the Crusaders marched was sealed between the towering walls. The landing zone was untouched.

Kondos whispered something.

'What did you say?' Narkissos asked. He couldn't hear her over the fading echoes of the metallic death of hope.

'They never bombed us,' she repeated.

'No, they didn't.' He struggled to his feet and wobbled down the rest of the ramp. There wasn't much left to do. A shedding of denial, a full acknowledgement of the scale of defeat, was perhaps the only trace of heroism that could still be claimed. He turned around, looking at the plain, at the hundreds of ships that had reached the star fortress. The fleet that the orks had allowed to come this far.

He looked up. There were great vessels at low anchor. He could see their lights. Two of those would be the ork cruisers. The others were the spoils of war, boarded and captured by the orks. Narkissos understood that the *Militant Fire*'s heroic run through the gauntlet had been a farce. The orks had boarded only those vessels which would not be able to make moonfall. They had let the others deliver themselves into their hands, and had destroyed the ones not worth their bother.

We gave them the Armada, he thought.

Stretching almost to the horizon, with only skeleton crews remaining, the ships waited for the conquerors to arrive.

They came while Narkissos stood there. Around the periphery of the plain, at the base of the metal mountains, the great doors opened, releasing the green tide.

Narkissos walked back to the ramp. He joined Kondos, and together they re-entered the ship. They closed her down, and retreated to the bridge, along with what crew remained. They armed themselves.

The struggle would be brief and futile, Narkissos knew. But he would die fighting. He wanted his life to have had that much meaning, at least.

The pounding began.

SEVENTEEN

Terra – the Imperial Palace

There was no scream. No cry. Now the time of the great silence had come. The eyes of the people of Terra had been on the ork moon. No one had expected to see the Crusade, though the collective imagination of the Emperor's subjects had landed with the Armada.

All who were watching saw the end of the Crusade. The movement of the mountains was visible from Terra. It looked like an eye closing, a wink, a mockery directed at its hapless prey.

Vangorich saw it happen from the Cerebrium. He was alone. The other High Lords were in session. They had remained in the Great Chamber for the length of the Crusade. The effort had been less heroic than they had expected. The war had lasted less than a day.

The movement seemed small on the surface of the planetoid. It was a minor rearrangement of its geography. Vangorich knew what it meant, though. He had told himself that he had nothing invested in Tull's folly. He was wrong.

He discovered that when he felt a vice crush something in his chest.

He thought of the reports that had come back about the star fortress over Ardamantua. How it had been a face. How it had spoken. He hadn't thought about the scale involved in such movement. He did now. He pictured being on the surface of the moon, of being caught in that collision of mountain chains.

Of being so insignificant that so small a gesture extinguished him.

He sighed and left the Cerebrium. He supposed he should be present for the end of the farce in the Great Chamber. He would bear witness. If Wienand, or a saviour not yet present in the Sol System, produced a miracle, then there would still be a reckoning.

He encountered the silence when he entered the Great Chamber. The parliament was as full as it had been at the launch of the Crusade. The assembly sat, robbed of volition. A hundred thousand servants of the Imperium, empty. There were some sobs. The weeping was so scattered and weak that it made the silence all the more palpable.

The stillness extended to the dais. Juskina Tull had been the presiding presence on the dais for the entire duration of the Crusade. As word of the landings had arrived, she had grown even more in stature, her energy of speech and gesture reaching for the superhuman. Now she was shrunken on herself. Her face, wan, seemed to vanish beneath the dead hand of her robes' glamour.

Vangorich thought of that moment, walking with Veritus in the aftermath of Tull's first speech, when he had contemplated the assassination of Tull and all the Lords who had stood with her. He had judged the move pointless. He believed he had been correct. Even so, he regretted the decision, and thought, I carry my portion of the day's shame.

The pict screens that had been installed around the dais showed static.

Vangorich mounted the dais. He evaluated the silence of the other High Lords. Tull's allies were as defeated as she was. Fabricator General Kubik was looking from static to static on the screens. Now and then, he uttered a short burst of binary cant, as if making notes to himself. Veritus looked thoughtful, but far from defeated.

'Are you going to share your optimism with the rest of the Senatorum, inquisitor?' Vangorich asked. 'Do you see a way forward?'

Veritus frowned. 'Your levity is misplaced,' he said.

'Is it?' He paused, then nodded. 'I believe you're right.' He turned his gaze on Tull and her allies. 'We've had enough of lunatic frivolities.'

The screen to the left of Udo's throne flickered back to life. 'It's Lansung,' the Lord Commander said.

Lansung's image steadied. 'We've picked up a signal,' he said. 'A ship has left the ork moon. It's on a trajectory for Terra.'

'The attack has begun?' Verreault asked.

'No. This is a single ship. It's Terran, and transmitting identification codes. It's a merchant vessel. The *Militant Fire.*'

'What is your recommendation, Lord High Admiral?' Vangorich asked.

'To let it arrive. This can't possibly be the invasion.'

'Then what is it?' Ekharth asked. The Master of the Administratum's cry was childlike.

It snapped Mesring from his catatonia. The glow of inspiration suffused his face. He stood up. He began to speak.

Encouraged by the Ecclesiarch, Ekharth's cry was taken up. It emerged from the silence, a reed-thin complaint from the depths of an echoing well. *What is it? What is it? What is it?* The news of the approaching ship rippled out from the Great Chamber to spread across Terra. The ship could be seen only by Terra's sensor arrays, but the haunted souls who stared at the moon imagined they could trace the path of the *Militant Fire*.

What is it? What is it? What is it?

Mesring's sermon fed the question. It offered no answers. It took theories apart. The orks were not attacking. The ship could not be a doomsday weapon, because it was too small, and what would be the point?

'Perhaps,' Mesring said, 'we are witness to a miracle. Perhaps, by the grace of the Father of Mankind, this blessed vessel has been delivered from our foe.'

An escape. The flight of a single ship could not offer true hope. But it was a dream.

What is it?

It is a sign.

The cry of frightened children was answered by a call to prayer. Summoned, the people came. Faith was the last refuge. They turned to it with a vengeance. The *Militant Fire* lay at the heart of the prayers. The people did not look to it for hope, but they prayed to the God-Emperor that it would become the source of hope.

In the Great Chamber, Mesring led the Senatorum in worship. Vangorich watched him with a mixture of contempt and admiration. Tull's moment had passed. The power dynamic of the High Lords had been in flux again with the failure of the Proletarian Crusade, and within minutes Mesring had the whip hand. Impressive. And pointless. How long did Mesring think the orks would allow him to enjoy his supremacy?

Mesring's sermon was not long. He gave the yearning of the populace a shape, then cast them back into a silence from which his voice would only be the more welcome when it returned. He sat down and bowed his head, his hands clasped.

Vangorich rose. He walked over to stand before the Ecclesiarch. 'Tell me,' he said. 'What if there is no miracle aboard that ship?'

Mesring looked up. He was calm as only a man who was as devout as he was devious could be. 'Then we will need our spiritual strength all the more.'

Vangorich swallowed his disgust and turned to Verreault. 'Is the Astra Militarum putting all of its trust into the divine?'

'A company of the Lucifer Blacks will meet the ship.'

'But not you.'

'My place is here.'

Of course it was. There might be more power plays in the time it would take for the *Fire* to arrive. The High Lords would be keeping each other under observation.

Vangorich left. All he would see here would be the rearranging of furniture in a burning house.

He made his way to the Daylight Wall. The Lucifer Blacks were attempting to take the place of the Imperial Fists. The sight of simple mortals in guard posts that had been manned by giants drove the loss home again. Vangorich spoke to the officer of the watch. The ship, he learned, was transmitting a request for permission to land at the Inner Palace's pocket space port. Vangorich considered the risk that the ship might be a bomb, come to wipe out the Terran leadership. The idea was so far removed from every aspect of the ork way of war that he snorted.

He passed through the gates of the Wall. He would meet the ship, and whatever news it brought.

The space port was not far beyond the Daylight Wall, and was visible from the High Gardens. It was reserved for high dignitaries from other systems and could accommodate a handful of lighters at a time. The *Militant Fire*, though a small merchant ship, was large for the space. When it arrived, Vangorich watched with approval as its pilot dropped the vessel between the spires of the Imperial Palace with an assured precision. Retro-rockets extinguished, exhaust from the descent dissipating into the grimy air of the palace, the ship sat in gathering silence for several minutes before a door rose on the port side of nose. A staircase descended. Then nothing more for a few minutes. The Lucifer Blacks' rifles were trained on the dark entranceway.

The figure that at last appeared was human enough. The man's clothes were expensive, though his coat was torn now. His face was grey with exhaustion and fear. He raised his arms over his head. 'My name is Leander Narkissos,' he said. 'Captain of the *Militant Fire*. Please don't shoot. No one on the ship is armed.' He waited, looking like a man who didn't particularly care if he was gunned down.

Vangorich walked forward on the landing pad and joined the commanding officer of the Lucifer Blacks. 'What is your name, captain?'

'Mercado, Grand Master.'

'The situation is tense, I know, and so are your troops. Unthinking fire is the last thing we need at this juncture, don't you agree?' He kept his voice calm, his tone light.

Mercado nodded. 'Hold fire,' he shouted. 'Weapons down, but keep them ready.'

'Come down,' Vangorich called to Narkissos, and he advanced until he was a few metres away from the base of the steps, visible to all the nervous soldiers.

Narkissos lowered his arms and took the stairs slowly. He wobbled when he reached the landing pad.

Vangorich stepped forward and steadied him. 'Did you escape?' he asked.

'No.' Narkissos looked back up at the doorway. 'They want to be escorted to the Senatorum.'

Vangorich followed his gaze. He almost asked, *Who?* but he knew the answer. Beneath the denial that even he maintained for the sake of his sanity, he had known since the ship's approach was first detected.

Three orks appeared. They descended the steps, and then they were there, on the landing pad, on Terra, near the heart of the Imperial Palace. Vangorich was not religious, yet his stomach turned at the obscenity of the greenskins' presence.

He fought down his atavistic response. He shouted 'Hold

your fire!' because the Lucifer Blacks would need to hear that command again. He forced himself to examine the orks so he, at least, might have some rational understanding of the Imperium's foe. He already knew he would be one of the few, apart from Kubik, to be capable of clear thought, and he didn't trust the Fabricator General to be candid with his insights.

Vangorich had studied all the reports the Mechanicus had made available about the resurgent orks. He had also read more than a few documents that the cult of the Omnissiah had preferred to keep to itself. One of the recurring themes of the studies, which the Mechanicus emphasised with undisguised enthusiasm, was novelty. These orks kept producing new weapons, acting in new ways. The pattern continued now. Vangorich looked at the orks before him, and felt another unwelcome shock of the new. All three were big. Two of them were a full head taller than he was. The third was half again as large. A leader and two subordinates, then. They wore thick leather, decorated with the brutal signs of the ork clans. The clothing seemed more like robes of office than armour.

What alarmed Vangorich most was not the unusual garb, though, but what the orks did not have.

They were unarmed.

Vangorich stared at this impossibility. The leader held a staff. It was three metres long, made of iron. Its girth was decorated with clusters of skulls. Some were human, others eldar, and many from species Vangorich didn't recognise. The skulls were iron also, their jaws agape in an agony of death. Real teeth hung from a coil of wire that spiralled the length of the staff. The crown was a representation of an ork face, snarling in victory and hunger. The staff was formidable, but it was not a weapon. By the standards of what Vangorich knew about the greenskins, it was an artistic masterpiece.

The orks watched him steadily. They were calm, motionless, and so even more disturbing.

All it would take on his part was a simple gesture. He could turn his head, nod at Mercado, and the orks would be gunned down.

The consequences of that choice, he knew, would not be pleasant.

'Follow me,' he said to Narkissos.

The Lucifer Blacks followed. He led a dark procession to the Great Chamber. Vangorich was conscious of every heavy step of the orks behind him. Xenos boots on Terran marble beat the rhythm of the Imperium's humiliation, and of the craven failure of the High Lords. He counted himself among the guilty. What did he have to show for his machinations? Playing host to the invader.

Narkissos walked like a man approaching his execution.

'Tell me who they are,' Vangorich said.

The trader whispered a terrible word. 'Ambassadors.'

'That isn't possible.'

'I know.'

So it was true, then. Vangorich felt colder inside with every passing moment.

Their arrival in the Great Chamber was greeted by a collective gasp followed by a growing murmur of rage. Udo rose from his seat. He pointed at Narkissos.

'What have you brought into this sacred place?' he thundered.

There was no threat in his bluster. He was an empty gesture given embodiment. Narkissos didn't flinch. He didn't even look at the Lord Commander. His eyes were unfocused. He was staring at something more vivid and frightening than the High Lords or the orks. A recent memory, perhaps, or a vision of the near future.

'They're ambassadors,' Vangorich said, the word alien in his mouth. He mounted the dais. The orks remained where they were. Their yellow, sunken eyes watched the High Lords. 'Are you their interpreter?' he asked Narkissos, wondering how the man had come to know the xenos tongue.

Narkissos looked up now. He shook his head, miserable.

'Don't need an interpreter,' the lead ork said. 'We tell you how to surrender, you surrender. Easy.'

EIGHTEEN

Terra – the Imperial Palace

The silence was as huge as the great scream had been. The scream had been the one response possible to the immensity of the moon's arrival. The silence was the one response possible to a few simple words. The earth did not shake. Walls did not topple. Yet it seemed to Vangorich that both events occurred with every syllable that came from the ork's mouth. Everything that the Imperium believed about the orks was wrong. The mere existence of these new orks, these ambassadors, was a blow whose implications were at least as great as the annihilation of the Proletarian Crusade. Here was proof that the military catastrophe was due to something more than brute power. The orks had numbers, and they had technology, and at least some of them had become a new thing.

Before the dreadful wonder of an ork dictating terms in fluent Gothic, what response could there be except silence? What emotion other than despair?

The ork had a name: Bezhrak. His Gothic was guttural. It sounded like the evisceration of prey. But there was no hesitation. Vangorich realised, to his horror, that Bezhrak spoke not as if he had learned the language of the Imperium, but as if it were his native tongue. The ork's expression was *uncultured*, and the fact that word even occurred to Vangorich was obscene. Bezhrak spoke as if he had spawned from a deep underhive.

'The Great Beast has you by the guts,' he said. 'Struggle, he'll rip 'em out. Surrender, you get to keep 'em.'

The silence stretched on.

Bezhrak looked around the Great Chamber. 'So?' he asked. 'Give up or die. Choose.'

The silence broke. The tiers erupted with screams, curses, wails of defiance and wails of despair. There were prayers to the God-Emperor, and there were what sounded to Vangorich like treasonous pleas for mercy directed at the orks. He tuned out the wider Senatorum. He was surrounded by enough idiocy on the High Lords' dais.

Mesring turned on Tull. 'What have you done?' he screamed at her. 'You have brought sacrilege into our midst. Holy Terra is defiled!'

'I didn't hear you voicing doubts earlier,' she retorted. She had regained some of her fire. She was in Mesring's face, giving no quarter, and standing with her back to the orks, as if she could erase the reality of their presence in a contest of rage with the Ecclesiarch.

Ekharth, Gibran, Sark and Anwar surrounded Verreault.

'Why are you silent?' Gibran asked, his voice rasping with hysteria. 'Give the orders! Kill the abominations!'

'The Lucifer Blacks outnumber them!' Sark sounded no better. 'They aren't armed!'

'And what does that tell you?' said Verreault.

That they're throwing our civilisation in our face, Vangorich thought. The self-inflicted moral wound the Imperium would suffer if it acted with less sophistication than orks would be a septic one.

The Master of the Astronomican was not worried about such concerns. 'Kill them!' Sark screamed. '*Kill them!*'

Bezhrak grinned at him. 'Bad plan, little bug.'

Sark paled. He sank back to his seat, trembling.

The Lucifer Blacks' rifles were still trained on the orks. The troopers' faces were strained masks of hatred. They did not fire. Verreault held up a hand, ensuring they did not.

'If we kill them, we sign our death warrants,' he said.

Udo sought refuge in bluster.

'We will not surrender!' he shouted at Bezhrak. 'We will annihilate your foul race. You have sealed your doom by coming here. You have...' he trailed off, seeking a greater curse. 'You will regret...' he began again, and stopped again, held by Bezhrak's gaze. 'I won't!' he yelled. 'We won't! You can't ever!' He descended into an incoherence of defiance. He was pathetic, Vangorich thought. Before long, he wouldn't even be howling words.

Kubik had advanced to the edge of the dais and was walking back and forth in front of the orks. He leaned forward, his telescopic vision lenses extending towards the trio. He was speaking quickly to himself. Vangorich doubted the Fabricator General experienced emotion in a recognisable sense. But there was something very like excitement in the flood of auto-dictation and binary. 'Not a clan. Specialised evolution is a defining characteristic of the *Veridi giganticus.* An ambassador class? An ambassador species? That might be closer. Yes, yes. Not learned behaviour. Diplomatic skills as genetic trait? Unprecedented. Specimen collection will be needed. And the potential. If the *Veridi* are capable of this form of development, mutations on command, the possibilities are–'

'Where are your loyalties, priest of Mars?' Veritus asked.

Kubik's neck twitched. He waved a multi-jointed hand, brushing away the irritation of the inquisitor's voice. He chattered in cant, already lost again in his speculations.

'Enough, then,' Veritus said. 'Bear witness, Father of Mankind,' he called out. 'I have tried. But they leave me no choice.' He stepped down from the dais. In his power armour, he was almost as wide as Bezhrak's attendants. He brushed past the orks and began the long walk out of the Great Chamber.

Vangorich watched him go. When he dropped his eyes from Veritus' retreating figure, he met Bezhrak's gaze. There he saw something that chilled him even more than the ork's use of Gothic: contempt. The two smaller orks were amused. They were grinning their disdain for the shrieking puppets on the dais. Bezhrak wasn't smiling. Vangorich didn't trust his ability to read ork physiognomy. He didn't want to trust it. He wanted to be wrong. Because Bezhrak's contempt appeared to be mixed with pity, and if that were true, what then?

What then?

Bezhrak raised his staff and brought it down against the marble floor. The reverberation was the toll of war. It brought a momentary silence to the dais. The High Lords faced the reality of their disgusted foe.

'Useless,' Bezhrak said. 'Worse than snotlings.' He looked at his fellows. 'No reasoning with humans. Break 'em, kill 'em, eat 'em. That's good. Don't try to make 'em think. Can't be done.' He shrugged. He turned back to the High Lords. 'Want to die, then? Last chance.'

The Twelve said nothing. Vangorich opened his mouth, and found he also had nothing to say. He had almost responded to an impulse to save face before the orks, and acting on that impulse would have been its own shame. And Udo was right, in his idiot blathering. There would be no surrender. There could be no negotiation. Before the ork that spoke, there could be no words.

Bezhrak gave him a long look, then nodded. 'So die,' he said. He brought the staff down again with a slam of judgement. He stood still and quiet, the fearsome focus of the Great Chamber.

Vangorich stared at the beast who had come to the heart of the Imperium and been repelled by the animals there. An ork had become the figure of dignity and, worse still, of *majesty* in humanity's parliament. With all honour dead, how was it possible that the ground did not open up and swallow the Palace?

To Narkissos, Bezhrak said, 'Done here.'

With Narkissos trailing them, the orks turned their backs on the High Lords of Terra. In their wake, the new silence continued. It was deep and painful as a terminal wound, but it didn't last. Words like blood poured from it, as the Lords turned on each other again.

We deserve it, Vangorich thought. The enormous, lethal, infinite foolishness of the human race shook the chamber and fell on his soul with the weight of a collapsing civilisation. We deserve it, he thought again.

He wasn't sure how long he stood there, staring at nothing, deafened by hopelessness. But he shook off the despair. He cast it away with a refrain. I will fight, he thought. I will fight.

I will fight.

He looked up. The orks were gone. So was the point of the Senatorum. There was nothing he could do here. There was nothing anyone could do here.

He wondered where Veritus had gone.

He had taken ten steps away from the dais when the explosion hit. It came from below. The floor of the Great Chamber shook and cracked. Tiers collapsed. The Imperium's futile dignitaries tumbled over each other in a human cascade. Tocsins competed with panicked screams. Vangorich ran towards the exit of the Great Chamber, where he saw Mercado yelling into a vox-handset. The captain looked up as Vangorich drew near. He lowered the vox-set. He was handling it as if it had bitten him.

'Is it the orks?' he asked. Had they somehow inserted a bomb beneath the Palace? Had he given them the opportunity to do so?

'No, Grand Master,' Mercado said. His voice was disbelieving. 'It's the eldar.'

ABOUT THE AUTHOR

David Annandale is the author of The Horus Heresy novel *The Damnation of Pythos*. He also writes the Yarrick series, consisting of the novella *Chains of Golgotha* and the novel *Imperial Creed* and *The Pyres of Armageddon*. For Space Marine Battles he has written *The Death of Antagonis* and *Overfiend*. He is a prolific writer of short fiction, including the novella *Mephiston: Lord of Death* and numerous short stories set in The Horus Heresy and Warhammer 40,000 universes. David lectures at a Canadian university, on subjects ranging from English literature to horror films and video games.

The Beast Arises continues in Book V

Throneworld
by Guy Haley
April 2016

Available from
blacklibrary.com and